# TALES OF FEYLAND AND FAERIE

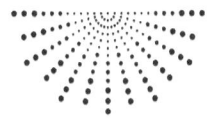

ANTHEA SHARP

Fiddlehead Press

Cover art by Ravven - ravven.com

Visit the author at www.antheasharp.com and join her mailing list for news of upcoming releases!

QUALITY CONTROL: If you encounter typos or formatting problems, please contact antheasharp@hotmail.com so they may be corrected.

Print ISBN: 9781680130447

# CONTENTS

*Dedicated to all the Feyland fans! Thanks for coming with me into the enchanted world behind the interface.*

～

# BENEATH THE KNOWE

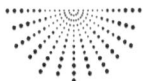

THE WIND off the white cliffs whipped Maeve Donnelly's hair about her face like ragged flicks of fire and tugged at the woolen shawl knotted around her shoulders. That same wind snatched the notes from her whistle, tearing the tune away from the hollow length of reed almost before her fingers could form the notes. Her rough brown skirts pressed against her legs, and high overhead, kestrels rode the currents. Could they hear her tune from where they floated, up there against the clouds?

Below the cliff-side, the sea crashed into rocks, white foam against dark water, tracing images she could almost decipher.

The wind veered, lashing her hair into her face and blowing straight into the fipple of her whistle, stealing the sound. Time and enough for her to stop. Her mother, Brigid, would be waiting for her to return with her basket of seaweed,

With chapped fingers, Maeve tucked her whistle into the secret pocket she had sewed for it in her skirts. If her parents saw the instrument, it would be trouble for her.

Had she anyplace else to go, or the means to get there, she would leave the small village of Dunkerry. But a young woman alone, with nary a skill to her name… well. She might be a fool, but she knew the bounds of her world clearly enough.

*And what of the music?* a small voice inside her whispered.

Ah, the music. Her bane and salvation, the tunes that bubbled through her, woven into the texture of her skin, the very beating of her blood.

Maeve sighed and shifted her basket to her other arm, stepping lightly over the hummocks of grass. Women did not have the bardic gift. She had been told that enough times, had humiliated herself by begging in front of the leader, Colm, and the entire clan.

"I have the music," she'd said. "Send me to the bards at Tara. Please."

"Prove it, then," Colm had said. "If the music flows in you as you claim, we shall hear it."

"I will." She'd pulled her first instrument from her pocket, the battered tin whistle she'd traded a traveling tinker her best shawl for.

Nobody knew she'd done it; she'd lied and said the shawl had been blown away into the sea. Every day for the past year, whenever she could steal away, she'd go over the Burren to practice. None to hear her but the tumbled gray stones and small white flowers, the tough grasses and the wide sky above. Rain or wind or blessed sun, she learned how to coax tunes from the hollow length of tin. She'd studied the whistle's construction, the way the fipple split and let air into the hollow length, the finger-holes placed just so. Although one was incorrectly drilled, making the tone a touch too low. Still, she'd learned to adjust her hand so that the note was true when she played it.

Finally, armed with a dozen sweet, bright tunes, she'd gone to her father. He'd laughed when she told him she had the bardic gift, and shook his head. When she'd insisted, he'd cuffed her on the shoulder.

"Be still," he'd said.

"Aidan." Her mother had laid her hand over his clenched fist. "Let the girl go to the leader. She won't be quit of this notion."

And so Maeve had gone before the clan at the next Gathering and made her claim. She'd pulled the whistle from her pocket, put it to her lips, and sent her music singing into the air.

Colm's eyes had narrowed, and he had traded a long look with her father.

"Anyone can blow a bit of air through a whistle," Colm said. "If you truly have bardic blood, you'd be able to do more than that."

He'd beckoned to the piper, Donal, who came forward and laid his heavy war-pipes in her arms. There was blunt sympathy in the musician's eyes, but he did nothing to aid her.

Maeve had tried to position the pipes correctly, but it was like holding a young, ungainly animal. The drones flopped and crossed, though she managed to hold the chanter at more or less the right angle. At last she'd stuffed the bag under her arm, nearly dropping the pipes in the process. The mouthpiece was too high for her, but she lifted her chin and puffed into it, filling the bag with air until she was nearly dizzy.

Then she squeezed, and the most horrific squawk emitted from the pipes, a screech and wail that set the whole clan to laughing. She squeezed again, her fingers desperately moving over the chanter, trying to make at least a semblance of a tune. Hot tears sparked at the corners of her eyes, but determination held them back. She would show them, she would prove herself.

But she could not produce anything except terrible sounds from the bagpipes.

The bag deflated with a last, weary groan, and Donal took the pipes from her unresisting grasp.

"Come, lass," her mother had said, laying an arm about her shoulders and steering her away from the laughter. "At least you tried."

Of course she'd failed on the pipes. They took *years* of practice to master, even for those with bardic blood. But no one would stand for her.

Her father had taken her whistle and made her watch as he threw it out over the cliffs. The thin shaft of metal had made a soft, breathy sound as it turned, end-over-end, and then plummeted into the waves with a splash she could scarcely see.

"That's done," her father said.

Still, the music itched and burned inside her. She hummed and diddled the tunes pushing at her, but they needed more—they needed an instrument. So she'd visited the salty marshes to the south on the pretext of picking berries, and harvested several long lengths of reed. It had taken weeks of whittling for her to make a whistle that even sounded a note, and weeks more to craft one that played sweetly and in tune.

Luckily, she had always been the one to volunteer to go out gathering, even in the worst of weather. Her absences could always be explained by a basket filled with mussels or berries or kelp.

Maeve crested the last hill. Her village lay below, bounded by green meadows and a stout palisade of logs and stone. The fortifications were not needed—there had been no raids, no invaders since long before her birth. For two generations, Dunkerry had been protected by other means. But that protection carried a price.

Maeve shivered and glanced over her shoulder. The Faerie Knowe rose to the north, near the edge of the cliffs. It seemed nothing more than a green hill, safe enough. Aye, but it was what lay under the hill that mattered; a gateway to the king-doms of the Fair Folk.

Hefting her basket, she set her steps toward the village. The gray houses and brown paths were softened by the thin drizzle in the air, and curls of peat smoke hung above the thatched roofs.

She paused before her cottage door, hearing the sounds of voices within.

"Tis past time to tell the girl," her father said, his voice raised in temper. "You've coddled her too long."

"She's not ready," her mother replied.

Fingers suddenly cold, Maeve set her basket down. They were speaking of her—they must be.

"Ready or no, Fergus will claim her as his wife at the next Gathering. Better it doesn't come as a surprise."

Shock stole her breath. Wife to Fergus? How could such a thing be?

She must have made a sound of protest, for her mother flung the door open. Brigid pressed her lips together and took Maeve by the arm.

"Don't stand out there in the wet," she said.

Maeve numbly grabbed the basked and let her mother tow her inside. Her father stood beside the hearth, his arms crossed.

"How could you?" Maeve asked. "How could you promise me to him?"

Fergus wasn't a bad man, but he was hard. Nor did she think he would treat her with any concern for her desires. Besides, he was a full ten years older than herself. When she dreamed of marriage, she had imagined someone nearer her own age, with gentle hands and kind eyes. Not Fergus.

"Your sister has been wed for two years now," her father said. "Past time for you to marry—and since you have taken too long about it, we've chosen for you. It's a good match. Fergus has the ear of Colm, and you will be a woman of influence."

"I won't!" Her protest rang out sharply.

"You will be wed to Fergus, or you'll have no home to go to at all. Think well on that, lass."

With stiff fingers, Maeve unknotted her damp shawl. The thought of wedding anyone, especially Fergus, was as bitter in her mouth as uncooked greens, and nothing would sweeten it. Half-formed plans darted through her, changing path midflight. She would go south, to the next clan's village, and hope they would take her in. But no, they would just hand her back to Colm. All the clans would. Well then, she would go and live wild on the Burren, scratching out a living from the stone. Or take refuge in a hidden cave beside the sea.

But she knew all her plans were useless.

"It will not be so terrible," her mother said at last, after the silence had stretched to breaking, and had broken, and then broken again.

Maeve hung her shawl beside the door. There was no comfort—there was only the difficult, impossible future ahead. No path led where she wanted to go. *Then you must make one*, a small, willful voice inside her insisted.

The clang of the alarm sounded outside, a high, insistent clamor. With a curse, her father took up his sword and strode out of the cottage, leaving the door open wide behind him. Chin high, Maeve followed. She could do nothing now, except set aside her own trouble and see what had raised the alarm.

In the center of the village, Colm stood with his bulky arms crossed. Beside him stood her sister Aoife, sobbing into her hands.

They had not been close, especially since Aoife wed the leader last year and bore him a son, but the sight of her sister's grief was a small knife through Maeve's heart. She hurried to Aoife and wrapped a comforting arm about her shoulders.

"What is it?" Maeve asked.

"My son!" Aoife cried. "They've taken him, curse those evil—"

"Quiet!" Colm's roar was nearly deafening. "Do you want to call more harm upon the clan? The warriors are arming even now. We will retrieve my son before night falls upon the land."

Maeve tightened her grip around her sister's shoulders

"The Fair Folk took him," Aoife said, her voice desolate. "They stole him from his cradle, and left naught but a gnarled stick and a handful of leaves in his place. They've taken him beneath the knowe, and I'll never see my sweet boy again."

She bowed her head, a fresh spate of tears wetting her rain-slick hands.

Maeve swallowed. Once a generation, the Fair Folk took a child. That was the price the village paid for living so near the Faerie Knowe and benefitting from its protection.

Nothing could be done—certainly not by force. It was beyond foolish for the men to attack the knowe. And yet, the leader's son had been stolen away. The village could not allow it.

"Assemble at the gates!" Colm cried.

The men of the village yelled and beat at their shields with newly-sharpened swords.

"Can they truly succeed?" Maeve asked her sister, not expecting a reply. "Come, I'll make you a tisane."

She led Aoife back to their parent's cottage, where no empty cradle awaited to spur another bout of weeping.

Their mother laid a new turve of peat on the hearth, and its comforting smoke and warmth soon filled the small living room. Maeve curled her hands about her own warm cup and regarded her sister's pale face. Deep in her heart, she knew that force of arms would not prevail against the Fair Folk.

But what would?

The afternoon seeped by in a gray haze. Aoife did not protest when Maeve led her to her own pallet and bade her rest. Though Maeve had no child of her own, she had already come to love her nephew's small softness, his tiny fingers and wide eyes.

Finally, near dusk, she could bear the inaction no longer. She pulled her brown shawl from the peg beside the door.

"I'm going to watch for the men," she said in reply to her mother's curious glance.

The rain had ceased and a thin line of pearly light etched the western horizon, burnishing the lip of the sea to silver. Maeve slipped her hand into her skirt pocket. Her fingers found the familiar shape of her whistle, and the seed of an impossible idea took root within her.

A thick clump of gorse grew beyond the village. Maeve knelt on the damp ground behind the prickly brushes, heedless of the wet seeping through her skirts, and waited for the men to return. If they saw her out so near sunset, they would insist she return to the village with them—and that she would not do.

Soon enough, she saw the score of warriors from Dunkerry returning from the direction of the Faerie Knowe. They straggled through the green grasses, supporting one-another. Several of the men were limping, and all had the defeated look of dogs sent home with their tails between their legs.

Maeve could not hear more than unhappy mutterings, but when they reached the palisade ringing the village, Colm raised his sword and shook it in the direction of the knowe.

"We will return," he cried. "And you will yield up my son—else we will sow salt upon your hill, and iron, and fire!"

The other men let out half-hearted *ayes*. Clearly they were not as eager as their leader to return to battling the Fair Folk.

Scowling, Colm strode into the village, Fergus at his side.

When the last of the warriors were gone, Maeve rose and hurried from her hiding place. Dusk was upon the land, that between-time when the gates between worlds were unlocked. She must make haste.

Taking up her skirt in both hands, she ran over the hillocks toward the rise of the knowe. Still, she did not run so quickly as to lose her breath; she must be able to play when she arrived.

The grass around the knowe was deep and lush, and seemingly untrampled, despite the earlier presence of the warriors. Maeve climbed to the top of the circular hill and stood there, looking out over the sea.

The last ray of sun speared from beneath the clouds, a brilliant shaft of orange that touched the water to a narrow path of flame. With a deep and steadying breath, she pulled the reed whistle from her pocket and brought it to her lips.

Clear and strong, she played the notes of the jig she had recently fashioned—a jaunty tune that swooped and soared like a lark in the blue air. Beneath her feet, she thought she felt the hill tremble.

Three times through the tune, and Maeve smoothly transitioned into another. A faster reel this time, the melody twisting and burbling like a stream over rounded rocks. The last bit of sun slipped below the horizon, and the notes of the whistle rang out, high and piercing and sweet.

With a groan and a rumble, a dark passage opened in the hill; a gaping mouth leading into darkness. Roots dangled from the curved roof, though the floor was paved in glimmering silver stones. A waft of warm air swirled up from the depths below, scented with delicate flowers.

Maeve finished the tune, the last line of melody suddenly sounding thin and forlorn. With cold and trembling fingers she slipped her whistle back into her pocket. She had guessed, had hoped, but now that her suspicions were proved true she did not want to follow where that passageway led. The Fair Folk were not for mere mortals to deal with.

*Think of the babe, she told herself. Think of Aoife.*

She could not enter the darkness under the hill for herself, but she could do it for them. Taking a last, deep breath of open air, she stepped onto the stones of the passageway. The floor sloped inexorably down, neither twisting nor turning. The floor shed a pale, steady light, even as the light of the mortal world faded behind her. After a hundred paces, Maeve glanced over her shoulder. There was only a small circle of dusk to mark the opening into the knowe.

"Halt," a deep voice said. "Who trespasses in the kingdom under the hill?"

Maeve clutched the frayed ends of her shawl and peered into the silver-lit shadows.

"I seek a stolen child," she said. She knew better than to give her name to the Fair Folk. They had enough power without her giving over the key to her true self.

A pale figure moved forward, clad in shimmering mail and carrying a long-hafted spear. His long hair flowed back from a high forehead, revealing pointed ears and an unearthly, handsome face.

"I am the Guardian of the Gate," the elfin knight said. "None may pass, without paying the price."

She had nothing to give—except her music. When she drew the reed whistle from her pocket, the knight laughed.

"We care not for such a plain trinket. Turn about, mortal girl, and leave the hill before it swallows you whole."

"I'm not giving you my whistle," Maeve said, irritation flowing through her like a strengthening tonic.

She brought the instrument to her mouth and began to play—a low, lilting air that had come to her from the quiet stones of the Burren, the solitary sun of a yellow flower before the storm.

The tune ended and the knight sighed, the sound sweet and ineffably weary.

"Very well," he said. "That will grant you passage to my king's court. I will summon a guide."

He lifted his hand, and a bright spark shone in the air. Maeve covered her eyes, the brightness printed on the back of her eyelids.

When she opened them again, a small figure stood beside the elfin knight. He came no higher than the knight's knee, and was clad in a tatter of wisps and leaves. His unruly hair was tangled about sharp-pointed features, and his smile was full of mischief, though Maeve saw no spark of ill-intent in his merry brown eyes.

"Greetings," the sprite said in a high, lilting voice. "I am Puck. Come, mortal maid, and see the wonders of The Bright Court. It is an honor bestowed upon few, to venture so far into this Realm."

A few steps beyond where the knight guarded the gate, the passageway opened into a misty cave. Archways and columns rose on either side, but Puck continued to lead her forward, finally stopping in front of a massive set of double doors. They rose into the mist, and seemed fashioned of pure gold, carved into sinuous designs: foliage, flowers, the figures of capering fey folk.

Slowly, without either herself or Puck touching them, the doors began to open. Radiance spilled from the widening crack, and Maeve squinted and turned her face away. Would she be entering the heart of a flame? For her nephew's sake, she would do it, though her heart beat fast and frightened at the thought.

The doors spread open, like shining wings, the too-bright

light faded, and Maeve felt her eyes widen at the sights beyond.

"Behold," Puck said. "The Bright Court."

He stepped over the threshold and beckoned her to follow. Fear and wonder warring within her, she did.

The Bright Court was, indeed bright as day. Tall trees shone gold and silver in the light, their branches glimmering with emerald leaves and brightly jeweled flowers. Underfoot, lush moss cushioned her footsteps, and the faintest brush of music caught at her ears.

Puck led her through the enchanted forest, the light growing brighter still. Something glowed high overhead. Maeve shaded her eyes with her hand and peered upward. It was not the sun, not here beneath the knowe. Instead, an enormous, luminous pearl hung, suspended on a silver chain. Its white radiance was touched with scarlet, as though ruby coals smoldered in the heart of that brightness. Such a light was never seen in the world above, nor would ever be.

"Yonder lies the true court of the Bright King," Puck said. "Take care, mortal maid."

Ahead lay a clearing full of glimmering figures: faerie women with gossamer wings, strange, spindly figures with overlong fingers, and small balls of light that darted hither and thither, stitching the air with brightness. The scent of roses filled Maeve's nose.

A dais rose in the center of the clearing, and on either side the Fair Folk reclined on couches fashioned of velvet and silk. Maeve's gaze snagged on one tall, ethereal woman, who held a blanket-wrapped bundle in her arms. Surely Maeve's nephew was swaddled within.

Atop the dais sat a throne of gold surrounded by glimmering grasses, and upon it was seated the Bright King. He was as perfectly formed as a sunbeam slicing across a midday lake, and his elfin beauty outshone even the bejeweled splendors of his court. His pale hair was swept back by a circlet of gold. Piercing silver eyes surveyed her from a face full of strength and otherworldly beauty.

Maeve caught her breath—for who needed breath in such a presence? It was enough simply to gaze upon him.

Then Puck pinched her leg with his sharp fingernails. The pain made her jump, but it was enough to clear the faerie glamour from her senses. She had not come here to stare, bedazzled, at the king.

"What have you brought me, Puck?" the king asked in a deep, rich voice.

"A maiden from the world above, your majesty," the sprite said, sweeping a bow.

He glanced sidelong at Maeve, and she hastily made the king a curtsey. The wool of her skirts were coarse and human against her hands. She felt like a speck of dirt in a honeycomb, dross surrounded by gold.

"Greetings, mortal girl," the king said in a low, rich voice. "What brings you under the hill?"

"I have come to take back something that belongs in the human world."

"If it is here, then it belongs to us," he said.

The look he gave her sent a prickle down her spine. Foolishly, she had not considered that she, too, might be trapped beneath the hill.

"I offer you a bargain," she said.

The watching courtiers leaned forward, their attention

sharp and focused. The king's brilliant eyes fixed up hers, and Maeve felt as though she were drowning in sunlight.

"A bargain?" he asked.

Tales of the Fair Folk often featured such things—though it was not always the human bargainer who was victorious in the end. They were tricky folk, and Maeve knew she would have to choose her words carefully if she wanted to win free and return with the babe to Dunkerry.

"Yes," she said, summoning up a bravery she did not feel. "I propose a trade. I will stay here for one night and play my music for you. In return, you will give me the human child you stole from my sister, and let me freely return to my village."

She pointed at the faerie woman with the quiet infant in her arms. It might not be a baby at all, but it was wrapped in the heather-blue blanket Aoife had woven for her new child. And Maeve had been very specific in her wording. She hoped she had not left something unsaid that would be her undoing.

The Bright King arched one elfin brow. "How do we know if your music is worthy enough to pay the price?"

"I'll give you a tune." Maeve pulled the reed whistle from her pocket.

Before fear could stiffen her fingers or worry steal her breath, she began to play. Bright notes filled the air, setting the leaves of the gemmed trees dancing, making the pearl high overhead glow with renewed brilliance. Maeve tossed the melody into the air like a bright streamer. Certainly the Fair Folk had magic and wealth and beauty—but they had never heard this tune before.

It had come to her, sweet and playful, as she watched the

children run and shriek in the high grasses. It was the music of simple pleasures, of mortal delight.

The court quieted. The king closed his eyes, a blissful expression stealing over the sharp planes of his face, and Maeve knew her bargain would be accepted.

SHE PLAYED the night through as the creatures of the Bright Court feasted and danced. Neither sup of food nor sip of drink did she take, mindful of the tales.

After what felt like hours, when her fingers were flagging and her cheeks sore, Puck swooped in before her, riding a snowy white owl. His eyes were bright, his hair tangled with the white stars of hawthorn blossoms. Jaunty, he leapt from his feathered mount and held a gleaming silver whistle out to her. The length shone like starlight, and a curling design of golden vines was embedded in the metal, each hole edged with a perfect, miniscule leaf.

"My lady bard," Puck said, no hint of derision in his high voice, "please accept this gift from the Bright Court."

Maeve reached for it—how could she not?—then hesitated. "Does this change our bargain in any way?"

"Fear not! Tis a gift freely given. Besides, it is for our own selfish pleasure." Puck winked at her. "We would hear your music played on a worthier instrument than the simple reed you now hold."

The new whistle was light and smooth under her fingers, and the tone was like honey and sunlight, if sunlight had a voice. The music issuing from it refreshed her, and the court as well, for the dancers swirled with new energy, laughter chiming up to echo in the gemmed branches. Even the king stepped down from his throne to dance with one of his gossamer courtiers.

Through it all, Maeve kept a small part of her aside, watching the blue bundle of her nephew. He was passed from creature to creature, and several times she saw his small fists waving above the blanket. Not once did he leave the confines of the court, and never did she see any ill intent directed at him.

Finally, the king raised his hands. Maeve finished the reel she was playing, and weariness crashed over her in a dark wave.

"My court," the Bright King said, "our long night of pleasure is at an end. Bring forth the babe, so that this mortal maid can be on her way. The bargain has been fulfilled."

A tall, willowy creature with pale wings and a sad smile stepped up to Maeve. In her arms she bore the child.

Maeve held out the silver whistle, though her heart ached to part with it. Still, she could not trade her nephew for something so small.

"No," the king said. "The whistle is yours now, as befits the music singing in your veins."

Clutching the instrument, Maeve made him a bow. "Your majesty is generous."

"Perhaps. Though perhaps you will not think so, soon enough." A hint of sorrow shaded his fathomless eyes. "Now, take the babe and be gone. And perhaps we shall meet again in another time and another place, maiden of Dunkerry."

As he spoke she felt a pull on her soul, a reminder of the power he held, and her own mortal insignificance.

Hurriedly, she slipped the silver whistle in her pocket, then took the warm bundle from the faerie woman. Her nephew looked about with his wide, unfocused gaze, and Maeve wondered how much of his journey under the hill he would recall.

"Come," Puck said. "Best that you do not linger here."

Wise words. Pulling the child close to her chest, she turned and followed the sprite. They passed though the bejeweled forest, the gold and silver leaves of the trees shimmering in an invisible breeze. The tall doors swung open at Puck's gesture. As soon as she stepped over the threshold, a chilly fog enveloped Maeve.

"Quickly!" Puck cried.

Taking hold of her skirts, he tugged her forward, past the misty arches framed by columns, the dim passages between leading to unknowable realms. Their feet made no sound on the silvery paving stones.

Nearly running, Maeve and Puck passed the figure of the faerie guard, who stood motionless as a statue as they hurried past. The pathway sloped up, and ahead Maeve could see the circle of sky. The pink and orange of dawn over the ocean was already turning to blue. The high chirping of swallows punctuated the air, and the smell of damp earth and salt was suddenly strong in her nose.

And then she was out, the babe safe in her arms. The sun surged above the ocean, and the green grasses of the Faerie Knowe bent in a mortal breeze about her feet.

"Follow your heart's music, young bard," Puck called from the recesses of the passageway. "Farewell!"

Maeve tucked the child close and raised one hand. The earth shut with a *whump*, the sod unmarked by any seam or hint of passage. The door under the hill was closed.

But she had her nephew, safe in her arms. And the silver whistle, a cherished weight in her skirt pocket.

The babe began to cry with the shrill wails of an infant in need of feeding. Murmuring hushes, Maeve sped down the knowe. She expected to see the warriors of the village returning this morn, steel in their hands and anger in their eyes, ready to win back their clan leader's son. But the green cliff-tops were empty of anything but the dipping swallows and the sound of the surf, crashing far below.

She topped the rise, and smiled at the village of Dunkerry below. They would be amazed to see that she, Maeve Donnelly, had succeeded where all the warriors had failed! She would use this victory to buy her way to the bards at Tara. If there were no women bards, well, she would be the first— but she suspected Colm had only said as much to dissuade her, and to keep her father satisfied.

The village looked strange to her eyes after the bedazzlement of the Bright Court. The scatter of cottages seemed changed, the palisade more weathered.

A man stood at the gate. As she drew close, Maeve made out his features: it was Fergus, but she scarcely recognized him. Deep lines seamed the sides of his mouth and his forehead, and he was bent, as if from age, over his sword.

"Halt," he said, one hand on his sword pommel. "State your name and business."

"It's me, Maeve. I've come back with Aoife and Colm's son."

"Maeve?" He leaned forward, eyes widening. "Maeve Donnelly? Where have you been these long years?"

"What?" Surprise tightened her fingers around the babe, and he let out an impatient squall.

"Thirteen years ago, to the day, you disappeared. Taken by the Fair Folk, just as Colm's son was. It is really you?"

"But… I only left last evening! I've not even been gone a day!"

Even as the protest left her mouth, she remembered the Bright King's cryptic words, the shadow of sorrow in his eyes as he accepted her bargain. One night under the hill—yet thirteen years had passed in the mortal world.

"Come," Fergus said. "We must see Colm."

He led her through the village. Whispers and gasps followed, and then Maeve heard a familiar voice cry her name.

"Maeve! My own daughter!" Her mother hastened from a nearby doorway.

"Mother," Maeve said, her voice trembling as she saw her mother's wrinkled features, her once-brown hair now white.

"*Mo cushla*." Brigid clung to her. "I thought you lost to me forever. After your father died, I was so alone."

"I never meant to be gone so long."

It had only been one night… but the proof of the years lay all around her. Her family was changed, her father dead with no farewell from his youngest daughter to speed him on his way. She felt cold, a chill of the soul that even the warmest day could not lift.

A small crowd formed about them, but they made way for Aoife. A girl clung to her hand, the child perhaps nine years old. Colm followed, his face grim.

"Aoife?" Maeve whispered.

Her sister's beauty had become gaunt and bitter, her proud face now sharpened by age and unhappiness.

Maeve lifted the bundle, and the babe waved his tiny fists again. "I've brought your son home."

Aoife took a step back, her mouth twisted. "I want no part of that changeling, or your fey magics. Look at you—still a maiden fair, while I have borne three children since, and seen two of them taken by winter fevers. Begone. We have no need of you here."

"But, your son…"

"Take him," Colm said to his wife. "We will find a wet nurse."

Unsmiling, Aoife snatched the babe from Maeve's arms. She looked down at him, and her expression softened slightly—a sight that gave Maeve some small hope for the child's future.

"Come back to the house." Brigid touched her shoulder. "'Tis better you give them time. Your return is so unexpected…"

Maeve had to shorten her steps to keep from outpacing her mother. Her throat still tight with disbelief, she blinked at the changes to Dunkerry, big and small. Half-familiar faces watched her from open doorways, children that she had minded now grown and married, some with children of their own. She stumbled over a patched bucket in the alley that surely had been gleaming and new only yesterday.

Their cottage was smaller and darker than she remembered, and quiet without her father's bluff presence. Maeve went to her pallet, then halted when she saw her corner was occupied by the spinning wheel.

"We'll make you up a bed," her mother said. "And surely Aoife has some clothing you can borrow."

"But where are my belongings?" The earthen floor tipped

beneath Maeve's feet. She felt overwhelmed by the changes, as though she was a swimmer in the rough ocean of time, the waves washing over her head. She was drowning, drowning.

"They are gone." Her mother's eyes held such sorrow. "There is nothing here that belongs to you. When you did not return, well... Your clothing and possessions were put to good use."

Of course. The village was not so wealthy that they would pack her few trinkets away in the vain hope she would one day return. The only thing she had that was truly hers was the silver whistle from beneath the knowe, nestled deep in her pocket.

If Colm saw it, rich and shining, he would take it from her. She must guard this secret well.

"May I rest?" she asked.

"Take my bed." Her mother pushed open the door to the bedroom and awkwardly patted Maeve's shoulder as she went past.

Her dreams were filled with brightness and melody. When she at last awoke and opened her eyes, Maeve nearly wept at the sight of the dim stones of the cottage walls. Lamplight cast a golden square through the doorway, and she could hear her mother at the spinning wheel.

"Ah," her mother said, when she saw Maeve at the threshold. "I've a bite of supper for you on the table."

Hunger knotting her stomach, Maeve sat and ate of the brown bread and cheese. At least the water from the village spring was unchanged; cool and faintly flavored with moss.

"What will I do?" she asked.

Brigid frowned at the spinning wheel, her fingers moving more slowly than they had used to. At last she spoke.

"You are a part of the village. They will make a place for you." Her voice was not as confident as it might be, and Maeve knew it would not be that simple.

Indeed, the next days were fraught with difficulty. All Maeve's old tasks had long-since been filled by others. A dark-haired lass scowled at her when she offered to take the girl's basket and collect seaweed in her stead, and the children ran from her, a stranger in their midst. Even Aoife turned her back when she saw Maeve coming. With the leader's wife showing her no favor, the rest of the villagers felt free to do the same.

Maeve was too much of a strangeness among them; a girl disappeared for thirteen years, yet not a day older. There was no place for her in Dunkerry—and from the sidelong looks and spiteful whispers, there would never be. The knowledge was ashes on her soul.

Finally, on a morning that dawned bright and clear, she collected the two worn dresses Aoife had begrudgingly given her, a knife and a cup, and her old shawl, and bundled them into a blanket.

"Must you go?" her mother asked.

"I don't belong here," Maeve said. In truth, she never had—always a lark among ravens. Still, her heart ached from it.

Eyes bright with tears, her mother gathered her into a tight embrace.

"I'll miss you so," she said. "But I have already mourned you once. And there is my grandson to thank you for."

"Look after him," Maeve said. She had not held the warm weight of the baby since handing him to Aoife.

"I'll gather you some provisions, some coin," Brigid said.

"Your father had a small store set by, and I want you take it. There is nothing in Dunkerry to spend it upon."

"I will send more," Maeve said, though she scarcely knew where she was going.

Word of her leaving had spread through the village, in the mysterious way such things do. When Maeve stepped out of the cottage into the sunshine, the street was lined with her former kin and clan. Some met her eyes and nodded, some would not look at her at all, but they all followed her down to the gate. There, Colm and Aoife waited.

"So, Maeve Donnelly," the leader said. "You think to make your way into the world?"

Beyond the open gate, swallows darted over the long grasses. The hush of the sea was borne on the wind, and the sun lay dazzling over stone and hill. For the first time since her return, Maeve felt a melody stirring within her breast.

"Yes," she said. She did not need nor crave his permission.

Aoife glanced down at her son, then at Maeve. Something softened in her expression, so that for a moment Maeve saw the young woman she remembered.

"Here," Aoife said, holding out a bracelet that gleamed gold in the sunlight. "Good luck, Maeve."

"*Adh mor ort,*" the villagers murmured, echoing Aoife's words.

"Thank you." Maeve took her sister's gift and fastened it around her own wrist. She would not sell it, unless her need was dire.

Her mother stepped forward to give her one last, fierce embrace, and then Maeve was free.

She slipped her hand into her pocket. The silver whistle lay cool against her fingers, a promise of her future. She would write a tune for Dunkerry—give voice to the longing and ache inside her, the chances missed, the years so suddenly spent.

Every journey must begin with a closing door.

"Farewell," she said, then turned her face to the east. Toward Tara.

# FAE HORSE

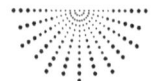

IF THE MEN CAUGHT HER, they would tie her to the stake and set the fire.

Eileen O'Reilly crouched beneath a hawthorn tree, her heartbeat dinning in her ears so loudly it nearly drowned out the sound of her pursuers. Torchlight smeared the night, casting fiendish shadows over the hedgerows. She clenched her hands in her woolen skirt and gasped for air, trying to haul breath into her shaking lungs.

She had heard there was no worse agony than burning alive.

The flames would scorch and blister her skin before devouring her, screaming, as her bones charred. Eileen swallowed back bile.

Shredded clouds passed over the face of the half moon. One moment, sheltering darkness beckoned; the next, the newly-planted fields were washed with silver, her safety snatched away.

"I see her—there, across the field!"

Cursing the fickle moon, and her fair hair, which had

surely given her away, Eileen leaped to her feet and ran. She crashed through a thicket, heedless of the thorns etching her skin with blood. In the distance she heard the pounding waves below the cliffs of Kilkeel.

Better a death by water than by flame. There was no other escape.

Five months ago, when the new vicar came to town with his fierce sermons and piercing gaze, she had not seen the danger. She'd lived in the village most of her life, first as apprentice to her aunt, then later taking on the duties of herb-woman and midwife.

But Reverend Dyer sowed fear and superstition—an easier harvest to reap than charity and love, to be sure.

Eileen stumbled, falling to her hands and knees in the soft soil. *Get up, keep running.* She must not give in, though her side ached as if a hot poker had been driven through it, and the air scraped her laboring lungs.

"There's no escape, witch!" The vicar's voice, deep and booming, resonated over the fields.

The stars above her blurred, and she tasted the salt of her own desperate tears. She risked a glance over her shoulder.

If she did not find a hiding place, they would catch her before she reached the cliffs. She veered toward the remains of the ancient stone circle that stood beyond the fields. Only two of the stones remained upright, the rest tumbled and broken. Still, she might find some shelter there.

She reached the ruin, and a figure loomed before her, large and dark. Lacking the breath to scream, Eileen staggered to a halt. What new enemy was this?

Four-legged and blacker than the shadows, it let out a soft

whicker. A horse, untethered, with a rope halter dangling from its neck.

Blessing her luck, Eileen caught the rope. It stung her hands, as though woven of nettles, but she did not care. Hope flared up, painfully bright. She might yet live to see the dawn.

"Easy now," she whispered, forcing back the panic pounding through her.

The horse was tall, and lacked any saddle or bridle. She gazed up at it and choked on misery. Her escape was in her hands, but she could not mount it unaided.

"Quick, lads!" the vicar bellowed.

*Now, she must go now.* For a strangled second she considered kicking the horse and holding fast to the rope, letting it drag her to her death.

A faint glimmer of gray caught her eye—a fallen stone tangled in the tall grasses. She tugged, and the horse followed her to the stone. Fingers trembling, trying to ignore the pounding footsteps of the men of Kilkeel, she scrambled onto the stone and pulled the horse close.

"Grab the witch!" That was Donal Miller, whose advances she had spurned. "She's summoned her familiar. Stop her!"

Torchlight flared orange and red against the horse's glossy hide. It rolled its eye, the white showing, and whinnied, high and strange.

The men were almost upon her. With a cry, Eileen tangled her hands in the horse's mane and heaved herself up.

"A devil steed! Catch it!"

As if only waiting for her to mount, the horse leaped forward. Hemmed in by the men, it let out a shrill whinny and rose up, hooves flashing. The coarse mane cut into her palms as she clung there, half falling. She must not slide off.

The horse stamped and feinted. She heard the thunk of hooves on flesh, and two of the men cried out in pain. Then they were through, bowling past the grasping hands and shouted curses. Eileen held on as the jolting pace smoothed into a gallop and the cries of the men grew distant.

Slowly, her breath returned, the stark edge of her fear blunted. She had escaped—for now.

But what of Aidan? His name was a knife through her chest.

Did her true love still live?

When Young Sean, the village simpleton, had come to tell her that Aidan had fallen into a fever, she'd gathered her herbs and charms and raced to the cottage he shared with his mother. The widow had grudgingly opened the door, her eyes narrowed in animosity. Eileen had handed the woman the herbs for a soothing tisane. Then, as planned, Young Sean caused a racket, freeing the widow's chickens and chasing them about the yard.

The moment Aidan's mother went to tend her fowl, Eileen darted into the cottage and rushed to Aidan's side. His dark hair was plastered with sweat to his forehead, and he shivered uncontrollably beneath the blankets. She dropped a kiss on his brow, flinching at the heat rising off him. As she slipped the charm over his neck, his skin scorching her hands, he mumbled. A coughing spasm shook him. When it finished he lay in a stupor, breath wheezing in and out of his lungs.

"Peace, *mo chroi*," she said, then softly wove the words to send him into a healing sleep.

'Twas perilous, to take a person to that between place, but Aidan was gravely ill. Even a few minutes of that enchanted rest would do much to ease the sickness. Her charm would protect him while his body fought for life.

However, if he slept too long the connection would fray, then break. Aidan's soul would slip free, and death would bear him away into the West.

She began singing the song to draw him back.

"Eileen," Young Sean whispered at the window. "Reverend Dyer is coming, fetched by the widow. Go!"

Fear stabbed through her, but she must remain. She must finish the song and draw Aidan back to the waking world.

"Witch!" The vicar slammed into the cottage and grabbed her by the hair.

Her scalp burned and tears pricked her eyes from the pain, but she continued to sing. Nearly done. One more phrase…

Reverend Dyer clapped a hand over her mouth, his skin stinking of onions. To ensure her silence, he pinched her nostrils shut. Eileen clawed at his arm, her cries muffled by his meaty palm.

"Do not think to ensnare me with your spells," he said.

"Cast her out," the widow cried, her face twisted with hatred. "Keep her away from my son."

"We will do better than that." The vicar grasped Eileen's arm, his fingers digging into her flesh. "We will burn her."

Panic gave her the strength to whip her head free. "No! You must let me wake Aidan. The danger—"

"Aiee!" The widow had gone to Aidan's side and spied Eileen's charm. Now it dangled from her wizened fingers, broken.

"Proof," she spat. "This evil creature has had dark designs on my boy since the day she set eyes upon him. Look, she has cursed him."

Eileen writhed in the vicar's grasp.

"He will die," she gasped. "I must—"

"Out!" the widow shrieked. "Take her!"

"I'll lock her in my cellar until the pyre is built," Reverend Dyer said, shoving Eileen before him.

She stumbled over the threshold, then caught her balance. Though she knew it was hopeless, she broke free of his grasp, gathered up her skirt, and ran.

The vicar would have retaken her, but for Young Sean. He threw a chicken at the vicar's face, granting her precious time to pelt from the yard. He would likely be whipped for it, poor man.

Now Aidan's spirit was in terrible danger, spinning out into the mist. She must turn her mount back toward the village and wake her beloved, before it was too late.

The black horse galloped madly through the night, avoiding every obstacle with uncanny precision. The ground blurred beneath them with sickening speed.

"Turn," she cried, yanking at the coarse mane.

Once. Twice. Thrice, until her hands stung, her muscles burning with effort.

The horse did not respond. Eileen might as well be a gnat on its hide for all the notice it paid. For one mad moment, she considered throwing herself off. But the risk was too great. She could not return to save Aidan if she broke her leg, or worse.

Over the thud of her mount's hooves come the boom and crash of the surf.

*Oh, no.*

They were racing straight for the cliffs. Ahead, the stars

were a veil reaching down past the horizon, disappearing into the dark Irish Sea.

"Stop! Please, stop." She pulled back with all her strength.

Her mount did not slow. Below them, the sea glimmered and heaved.

Eileen tried to release the horse's mane, but the strands were wrapped tightly around her fingers.

"Let me go!"

Heart pounding, she yanked. Her hands would not come free. She attempted to leap off, but her legs were bound fast to the horse's sides. She screamed and thrashed in panic, banging her elbows against the horse's shoulders.

They reached the cliff's edge.

Eileen's stomach churned as grass turned to empty air. Then they were falling, plummeting to their doom.

She found that, after all, she rather desperately wanted to live.

The water swirled restlessly beneath them. Eileen squeezed her eyes shut. She could not bear to watch the surface coming closer, closer. Or worse, the teeth of the hungry rocks, waiting to crush her body and spit it into the sea.

They hit the water with a crash. She gulped in a breath as the sea grabbed her legs, her arms, then closed relentlessly over her head.

She tightened her legs around the horse, the only warm thing in a world of shivering salt. Its withers bunched as it swam. They must be close to the surface. They *must*.

Lungs clenching with the need to breathe, she tipped her head back and opened her eyes, blinking past the sting and blur.

The wavering moon lapped the water, high overhead. The horse was not struggling toward the surface. Betraying its fey nature, it swam strongly downward, untroubled by the need for air. The surface glimmered, receding, and she could not free herself.

So, it was to be death by drowning after all.

Eileen released her breath in a silver stream of bubbles. They raced away from her lips, uncatchable. Crying, though she could not feel the tears, she laid her cheek against the water horse's neck. In another moment, she must gulp in the harsh tang of salt water. It would fill her, smother her—but at least it would be a quick end.

"You are brave, for a human." The words sounded in her head, the voice low and amused.

It was the uncanny creature she rode, speaking to her; or it was her own mind, conjuring up visions as she descended into her doom.

"Release me!" She aimed the thought at the black head bobbing through the water in front of her. "Or do you want a sodden corpse bound to your back for a blanket?"

She must breathe—her body demanded air. Against her will, Eileen's mouth opened and she gasped in the cold seawater. Choking, she doubled over on the horse's back as the water invaded the warmth of her throat and stopped her lungs.

Cold, and bitter, the weight of the sea lay heavy on her chest. She was dimly aware of silver spattering the surface above her head.

Then, with a thrust, the horse burst into the air, spray flying in a mighty gout. Eileen leaned over her mount's neck and heaved up water. She coughed and vomited, the agony in her lungs like a thousand stabbing pins.

Finally, teeth chattering and fingers numb, she pulled in a breath of sweet, sweet air. The horse bore her strongly through the heavy wash of the sea, no longer seeming intent on drowning her.

"Thank you," she whispered into its thick, black mane.

Her mount veered, swimming toward the rocky beach. Low, shadowed hills rose behind, and further down the coast the cliffs shone. Eileen coughed again and huddled against the horse's burning heat as the waves shoved against her.

"Do not thank me yet, human girl," came the reply. "The night is not ended."

The voice she'd heard beneath the water had not been her imagination. It held the echo of terror, a darkness she did not want to heed too closely.

"What are you?" she asked. "A kelpie?"

Even as she spoke the word, she knew it to be untrue. A kelpie would have taken her directly to the bottom of the sea, delighting in the drowning.

"Nay."

"Then you are a *púca*."

Her aunt had raised her on tales of the fair folk. Indeed, she should have realized her peril far sooner, but fear had blinded her in one eye, and hope in the other.

"Not just any *púca*. I am Tromluí, shredder of sanity, waker in the night. The longer you remain astride me, the more of your mortal soul you will lose. You should have chosen drowning, girl."

Eileen shuddered, cold to her marrow.

Better to be trapped on a kelpie's back. But no, she was

astride the NightMare. She might live to see the dawn, but only as a madwoman, chased by stones and suspicion from village to village, cackling in the grip of her lunatic visions.

The mare strode up from the sea, hooves clattering against the stones of the beach. Overhead, the half moon shone, a bowl of whitest milk. At first the air seemed warm, but in moments Eileen's skin prickled with gooseflesh. Her hair hung in a soggy plait down her back and saltwater dripped into her face, stinging her eyes.

"Will you let me go?" she asked, despairing at the answer.

"Shall I?" The mare's voice was ice and midnight. "I might climb into the stars and release you there, high above the earth. For a short time you would know what it is to fly."

The copper taste of desperation flavored Eileen's mouth. Indeed, she rode a dreadful creature. But she was not dead. Not yet.

Possibilities, sharp and painful, brought her upright, her mind racing. It was perilous to bargain with the fey folk—beyond perilous—but this night was full of wild chance. Already she had escaped death by fire, then by water.

"I will remain upon your back," she said. "But I demand a boon."

The NightMare turned her neck, regarding Eileen with an eye the color of moonbeams.

"It amuses me to hear your request. What is it you desire?"

Eileen swallowed and forced her voice to steadiness. "Help me save my beloved, Aidan."

She had sent his soul spinning from his body, and she must return it. No matter how dire the consequences.

"This is no small thing you ask," the mare said. "There will be a price, mortal."

"I will pay," Eileen said recklessly.

The horse gave a high whinny. Through the clear, still air Eileen heard the ring of chimes.

"Our bargain is sealed," the mare said. "Now hold fast, for we have far to journey 'ere the sun rises."

The NightMare leaped forward, muscles bunching beneath Eileen's legs. The rocky clatter of the beach fell behind as the mare galloped up the long rise of hills, leaping low stone walls and skirting tangles of briars. Eileen ceased shivering as the night wind dried her dress and the Night-Mare's heat seeped into her body.

With every stride, something burned away in Eileen's blood. She could feel her earliest memories shred and tatter, but she clung tightly to every thought of Aidan.

Near the top of the highest hill, the mare slowed, her hoof beats no longer the frantic race of a pulse but the slow stutter of a dying heart. A dark maw gaped in the side of the hill; the doorway to a barrow grave. Starlight picked out the gray stones outlining the opening, but within was sheer blackness.

As if aware of their presence, a dank wind moved from the depths of that hole. Eileen, her hands freed from the Night-Mare's mane, covered her nose at the stench of old, dead things.

A large, flat stone scribed with spirals marked the threshold. The mare raised one hoof and brought it sharply down upon the stone. Bright sparks skittered, followed by a distant, booming echo. Twice more the mare knocked, and each time the sound grew closer, until it vibrated Eileen's very bones.

The air of the doorway wavered, like a pond stirred by the wind.

"We pass now into the Realm," the NightMare said. "You

must remain on my back, no matter the sights you see or the danger you face. Are you ready?"

"Yes." The syllable floated up from Eileen's mouth, a fragile moth lost in the night.

The mare stepped forward. As they passed over the threshold, Eileen felt a terrible pain, as though angry wasps swarmed over her. She bit her lip and drove her fingernails into her palms, determined not to cry out.

Inside the barrow a pallid light spread, illuminating a stone-lined corridor with a corbelled roof. Rank fungus, pale and misshapen, grew along the edge of the flagstone floor and clumped in crevices on the walls. The stinging pain passed, but the clammy air lay heavy against her skin.

She cast a look over her shoulder, straining for one last glimpse of the night sky before the mare bore her deeper in. The stars were tiny pricks of light, washed dim by the moon. Then the opening was blocked by a shambling figure. The barrow light illuminated its skeletal form, ancient skin shriveled tight against the bone. Tattered rags hung from its limbs and a golden torc encircled its neck, marking it as a chieftain of yore.

From the skull-like face, empty sockets regarded her. Deep within lurked a spark of eldritch fire. The corpse opened its mouth in a soundless laugh.

Eileen pivoted away and leaned over the mare's neck, hoping her mount might hurry, but the NightMare continued her measured pace down the corridor. Another memory untangled itself from Eileen's mind, flared and burned down to ash.

The echo of hoof beats was soon muted by the slither and scrape of dozens of footsteps.

Throat dry, Eileen glanced behind her again, and smothered a scream. The dead followed, patient in their stalking. *Your beloved will soon join us*, their tongueless mouths seemed to say.

"No," she whispered.

The barrow amplified the sound, turning it into a long *"ohhh"* of despair.

"Quiet," the mare said. "Or do you wish to bring the *bean sidhe* for a visit as well?"

Eileen had been afraid before, but this slow, creeping terror held her nearly paralyzed. What if the NightMare chose to stop and allow the restless corpses to touch her with their rotting fingers? Would they merely stroke the resilience of her living flesh, or would they gouge great handfuls, feasting on her in a vain bid to regain their own vitality?

From the avid lights in their eye sockets, she very much feared the latter.

The mare bore her past an opening to her left, filled with the tang of blood and the sighing of the sea. Then an opening to her right, where noxious vapors swirled. Eyes stinging, Eileen buried her face in the crook of her elbow and tried not to inhale. Her heart beat hard and fast, knocking against the fragile prison of her ribs.

She did not need to look back to hear the following dead.

At length, her mount brought her to the central chamber. The pale light revealed crumbling treasures in the corners: rotted linens, tarnished silver set with dully gleaming gems, a golden goblet with one side crushed in as though it had been used as a weapon in some vicious fight.

In the center of the room lay a stone slab, and upon that slab...

"Aidan!"

She swung her leg over the mare's broad back, and only a shrill whinny of warning made her halt. Mere inches from dismounting, Eileen scrabbled back onto the horse. The dead hissed in disappointment behind her.

Hands trembling with impatience, she forced herself to be still as the NightMare stepped up to the slab.

Aidan lay as if asleep—or lifeless. His eyes were closed, and he was dressed in the raiment of an ancient king, with gold armbands encircling his biceps and thin circlet set upon his brow.

Digging her fingernails into her palms, Eileen watched his chest, straining for a sign of breath. At last, it rose in a long, slow inhalation. She slumped back, tears pricking her eyes.

"He lives," she whispered.

"Not for long," the mare replied. "You may step down now, but stay upon the marble verge. Should your foot touch the flagstones, you will be lost, and your love as well."

Eileen slipped down, placing her feet with care. She cupped Aidan's cheek.

"Wake, beloved," she said.

He made no response.

"Aidan, please wake."

She took his shoulders and shook him, gently at first, then harder as he continued his enchanted slumber. A kiss did not wake him, nor a shout. The echoes of her cry woke strange shadows that skittered across the ceiling, but Aidan slept on.

Throat choked with tears, she turned to the mare. "What shall I do?"

"He has dreamed too long, too far from the mortal world. *Tír na nÓg* calls to him strongly."

As if confirming the words, the dead lined up in the chamber stirred and rustled. The fallen chieftain took a step forward. Soon, Aidan would be among their number.

*No.* She refused to let him slip away.

Eileen gazed at his strong, beloved face. Her heart had long belonged to Aidan, since the first time she met him while picking herbs. He was brave and kind, and deserved a long, full life. And he was lost to her, now, whether she lived or died.

"Lie beside him on the slab," the mare said, "and take his hand."

The stone chilled her side, but Aidan's fingers were warm in hers. She watched the excruciatingly slow rise and fall of his chest. With one finger she traced the slope of his nose, the line of his jaw.

She must sing him back.

Pulling in a breath of grave-cold air, she began. His spirit had traveled far down the road to the West, and the simple waking chant would not be enough. It must be a call home, back to the human world.

Her voice filled the chamber as she sang the heat of summer, the call of the thrush, the taste of ripe berries on the tongue. Every warm, vital memory she once owned, she gave to him, spilling it forth. Each word carried more of her humanity out of the shell of her body and into his. The golden plait over her shoulder leached of color, the strands turning an eerie white.

Slowly, the dead began to dissipate, fading under that mortal onslaught.

Eileen sang of fresh-baked bread, a child's laughter. The

humming feel of her hand clasped in his as they laughed together above the ripening fields.

Aidan's breathing sped, his cheeks flushed with warmth and color.

Three of the dead remained. Then two. Then only the chieftain. It stared at her, bony fingers wrapped around the golden torc at its neck. The cold malevolence of its will dampened the song, chilled the air to ice.

Shivers gripped her, but she raised her voice, defiant. This time, nothing would stop her.

The last syllables faded. The dead chieftain took another step forward, and Eileen caught her breath. Had she failed?

Then Aidan opened his eyes. Turning his head, he smiled at her so freely she felt her heart break in two. From that crack, the last of her mortal essence seeped. The dark form of the NightMare struck her hoof against the slab.

"Eileen?" Aidan asked, blue eyes clouded with confusion.

"Live well," she said. "Live long, and happily. I will never forget you."

"Why would you need to? I'm here, beside you."

She shook her head, her chest aching with sorrow. "There is no future between us, my love. We must part."

"No! Marry me, I don't care about—"

She stopped his words with her lips, a last kiss to carry her into the night. He tasted of apples and sunlight; everything now lost to her.

The dead chieftain howled. The mare's hoof boomed against the stone. And between one heartbeat and the next, Aidan was gone.

Weeping, Eileen bent her forehead to her knees. The

breath of the NightMare was hot upon her nape and the stone beneath her wet with salt, with blood.

Yet she remained.

Wondering, she sat and lifted her hand, curling her long, wraithlike fingers. Had she a mirror, the reflection would bear little resemblance to the human features she had once called her own.

"The price has been paid," the NightMare said. "And I have a new rider. Come."

The far wall of the barrow clattered down to reveal a night rich with shadows and starlight, and a wild, fey wind that called them to ride.

Eileen-that-was rose from the stone, her body hollowed nearly weightless, freed of memory, freed of hope. She mounted the black horse.

Together, they flew forward into that sweet dark.

~

# BREAKING THE BROWNIE CODE

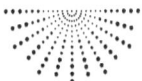

IT WASN'T A SIMPLE THING, cleaning a cottage in a wink while the humans slumbered. And to be honest, Feeyah MacGuire was not the most accomplished of brownies—as her boss, Biddy Porter, was even now pointing out.

"There's enough dust beneath the bed to fill a frying pan," Biddy said sternly. "The kettle isn't nearly polished enough, and I found a large spot of jam on the countertop. Feeyah, you're a disgrace to the profession."

Feeyah dropped her gaze to the pointed tips of her leather slippers. Shame and a tiny bit of anger mixed hotly in her blood.

"I didn't ask to be born a brownie," she said.

It didn't help matters that she was allergic to dust, and too much scrubbing made the skin of her hands red and itchy. She loathed the fact that she was compelled to rise well before sunup to scrub and sweep and polish and tidy, and her only reward was a sip of milk from a wooden bowl. She usually was the last brownie to finish her chores, and so got the last bit of milk—barely a mouthful. Sometimes less, if the others were greedy.

"Fix your hair and finish up," Biddy said, with a disapproving look at the wisps that had escaped from Feeyah's bun. "I'll be back to check your work, and this cottage had best be neat as a pin. Don't forget to tidy up the child's blocks."

Biddy glanced at the corner where the child slept, a scattering of wooden blocks on the slate floor around his bed.

"Yes'm," Feeyah said.

Truly, what else could she do?

Despite her complete ineptness at cleaning, she had the call in her blood. Oh, she'd tried to ignore the compulsion that woke her from her warm dreams into the cold wee hours of the night, but it was an itch that became a red-hot goad if she did not rise and join the other brownies at their work.

She had considered running away from the clan to seek a different life. Perhaps, once she left the Big People's house, fled from the hidden brownie dwellings and the company of her own kind, she would be free.

But a brownie alone was easy prey for foxes and other creatures. Without a safe haven to go to, she wouldn't last one night outside by herself. If the animals didn't eat her, there were other, darker folk who would find much sport in tormenting a mild-mannered brownie: the spriggans with their long, pointed nails, the redcap goblins who delighted in pain and mayhem, the malicious sprites who fed off of fear.

Despite her unhappiness, the clan would keep her safe.

Feeyah heaved a sigh, then took her broom and ducked under the bed. The dust made her sneeze, but brownie magic kept her from waking the humans who snored above her. More's the pity.

And yet... what if she tried to deliberately rouse them?

It was a daring, dreadful thought, but as she swept, the notion would not let her go. She finished her sweeping and magicked away the broom and dustpan. Heart pounding, she poked the loose strands of her plain brown hair back into her bun, then went to the foot of the bed and let herself rise up. Brownies could levitate themselves—how else could they dust the cobwebs from the rafters and reach the difficult corners behind the stove?

She wobbled a bit, and grabbed at the bedpost to steady herself in the air. It was one thing to use her magic for cleaning, and another altogether to attempt to meddle with mortal folk. Carefully, she landed on the wool blanket beside the wife's feet. The sleeping lumps of the humans rose before her like low hills.

Oh, but this was wicked of her. Brownies were not to be seen by mortal eyes. It was one of the most important points of the Brownie Code. But Feeyah was so bone-weary of her tasks, she was willing to break the code.

If the Big People saw her, what then?

She did not know—had only had heard dire whisperings and half-told tales. But certainly everything would change. It must, for she could not keep scraping along in misery.

Breath fluttering in her lungs, she crept alongside the sleeping wife until she stood beside the pillow. The woman's chest rose up and down in her dreaming, like the surface of the sea, and her face was smoothed of cares. Feeyah lifted her hand, and—

"Feeyah! Hist, away with you!" Biddy materialized beside her, wrapped her stout arms about Feeyah's waist, and pulled her to the floor.

They landed with a bump on the flagstones, and Feeyah pulled out of Biddy's grasp.

"Whatever were you thinking?" Biddy's gaze was hard as ice.

"I just... I wanted..." The words clogged in Feeyah's throat.

"You're perilously close to trouble, young miss," Biddy glanced over to the kitchen. "The kettle is still tarnished. If you don't get back to work, there'll be no milk left for you at all. Is that what you want?"

Feeyah shook her head, tears prickling hotly at the corners of her eyes.

"I'm not fit for the work," she said in a low voice.

"Of course you are." Biddy straightened her apron. "You're a brownie, after all. Now back at it."

She made a shooing motion with her hands, and Feeyah glumly levitated herself up to the kitchen counters. She conjured a scrap of linen and a dab of polish and set to work on the kettle. Half of the metal cleaned up fine, but as Feeyah kept working she ended up smearing soot back over the part she had already polished.

She fetched a new rag, but try as she might, the blasted kettle would not stay clean and unsmudged.

Perhaps she needed a little water from the basin in the sink. She trudged over the counters, not watching her step, and her shoe stuck fast in the spot of jam she'd neglected to scrub. Her rag went flying and down she went, hands before her to break her fall.

A hot flash of pain in her wrist made her cry out, and the sleeping couple mumbled in their dreams. But they didn't wake.

Feeyah sat cross-legged on the counter, wrist cradled in her lap while tears washed her face. Oh, she was most useless, clumsy brownie who had ever lived. Perhaps she *would* slip out at dawn, alone into the wide and terrifying world, and let her fate take her. The clan would be glad enough to be rid of her.

"Why're you crying?" It was a quiet voice, but unmistakably human.

She darted her head up. The child had woken, and was sitting up in his small bed at the far side of the room, looking directly at her. He slipped from between the covers and padded over to the kitchen. A youngling still, his nose came to just above the countertops, and his dark hair stood up in dream-tangled tufts.

"Can you see me, then?" Feeyah hiccupped back her tears and wiped her eyes with the back of her uninjured hand.

"Of course. Seen you lots of times," the boy said in a matter-of-fact tone. "Did you hurt yourself?"

She blinked at him a moment, trying to absorb the fact that the boy had seen her—with no measurable consequences whatsoever. So much for her thought of waking his parents. So much for the notion that being seen by humans would change anything.

"Aye," she said after a moment. "Twisted me wrist."

"Stay here," the boy said, his face lighting. "I'll help you."

He darted back to his bed and pulled out a worn stuffed bear with a kerchief fastened about one fuzzy leg. The boy fumbled at the knots, then pulled the linen free and hurried back to where Feeyah sat.

"I'm a good doctor," he said. "Bumble's leg is all better now, so you can use his bandage. We'll make you a sling."

He tied two corners together in a clumsy knot and held it up.

"Come closer," he said.

Feeyah stood, then hesitated. Was this a trap? But the boy's brown eyes were clear and guileless. Swallowing past the lump of fear in her throat, she went to the edge of the counter, then ducked her head and let the boy slip the makeshift sling over her head.

Even though it was a small kerchief, the corners hung down past her knees. She was certain she must look ridiculous.

"Better?" the boy asked.

"Aye."

Her wrist still throbbed, but his kindness warmed her. And she had to admit her arm felt a touch better inside the support of the cloth.

A flicker of motion caught her eye, and she saw Biddy waving urgently to her from behind the butter churn. The older brownie was scowling, with a look fierce enough to strike moths from the air.

"You'd best be getting back into your bed," Feeyah said to the boy.

Disappointment shadowed his face. "Maybe... maybe when you feel better you could come and play with me?"

"Perhaps I shall." She owed the child a debt of kindness now, and faeries always paid their obligations. "Back to dreaming you go, young lad."

"My name's Ian," he said. "What's yours?"

Biddy shook her head violently, and Feeyah narrowed her eyes. She might be a poor excuse for a brownie, but she was not fool enough to give away her true name.

"You can call me Fee," she said. "Good night."

Biddy lifted her palm and blew an invisible puff of slumberdust at the boy. He yawned, then turned and, without another word, climbed back beneath the covers. In moments his eyes had closed and his chest rose and fell with the even breaths of sleep.

"Feeyah MacGuire!" Biddy stormed out from her hiding place, her voice sharp with wrath. She fetched up before Feeyah, sparks nearly crackling off her small form, and jammed her hands on her hips.

"I didn't mean to—" Feeyah began.

"Just look at you! Speaking with a human, and—worst of all—accepting clothing from him. Oh, you've done more than broken the code, girl, you've shattered it completely."

Feeyah plucked at the sling fastened about her neck, her arguments dissolving at the tip of her tongue. It might not have been meant that way, but the truth of the matter was that a kerchief was, indeed, an item of clothing.

Which meant...

"Am I free, then?" The thought trembled against her heart, exhilarating and alarming.

"The council will have to take it up." Biddy blew an irritated breath from her nostrils. "Now come along. Clearly you can work no more today."

Feeyah cast a last look at the sleeping boy. Gratitude flashed through her, overriding the throbbing pain in her wrist. Then she meekly turned and followed Biddy back to the hidden brownie enclave.

～

FIRELIGHT FLICKERED over the seamed faces of the brownie leaders. The three elders of the council sat in ornately carved wooden chairs before the wide hearth in the common room. Feeyah stood on the flagstones before them, feeling like a fawn before a pack of wolves.

Old Tuck puffed away at his pipe, Eilis knitted on the endless scarf she always had in her lap, and Seamus narrowed his stone-gray eyes at Feeyah. His gaze flicked down to the sling she wore, then back up to her face.

"It cannot be denied," he said in his gravelly voice. "Feeyah MacGuire has accepted a gift of clothing from a human, and is no longer bound to serve in the household."

"What's to be done with her?" Old Tuck asked, blowing a smoke ring to punctuate the question.

Feeyah clenched her uninjured hand, wishing she could ask for mercy. But she was guilty as charged, and to speak now meant her punishment would be even more severe. Fear gripped her in its sharp jaws as she thought of what the consequences of breaking the Brownie Code might be.

"Send her to the Drummond clan," Eilis said. Her needles clacked in time to the words. "If she survives the journey, they'll take her in."

"Feeyah's my wife's cousin's niece," Seamus said. "I can't just expel her and force the lass to make her way in the world."

"She'll be eaten up in a trice." Old Tuck laughed, as if the idea amused him.

Feeyah shivered. So, it was to be the foxes and goblins, after all.

"Oh, stop it." Eilis set her needles down and fixed Old Tuck with a glare. "You're frightening the lass."

"She deserves it, too," Seamus said. "Imagine, letting a human see her."

"The boy said he'd seen me before," Feeyah blurted. "Many times."

Three sets of wise old eyes turned upon her, and she wished the floor would swallow her up.

"Did he now?" There was a mildness in Seamus's voice she knew better than to trust.

"That surprises me not a bit," Eilis said.

"Hmph." Old Tuck took another puff on his pipe. "I suppose what's done cannot be undone. Clearly the boy can hold his tongue."

"Tell me." Seamus leaned forward, his wooden chair creaking. "Did the boy ask anything of you?"

"Yes," Feeyah said, her throat so dry she could scarcely form the words. She paused to swallow.

"Well? Out with it," Old Tuck demanded.

"He... he asked if I might come play with him, once my wrist healed," she said.

"Ha!" Eilis cackled. "Clever lad, that. You're bound to do so, my girl, do you understand?"

"Aye," Feeyah said.

"That's settled, then," Seamus said. "You'll have to remain with the clan. Now, where's my ale?"

It was a clear dismissal. Feeyah curtsied to the elders. Old Tuck frowned, as though she had gotten off far too lightly, but Eilis gave her a sly wink. Seamus just waved her away as if she were a buzzing gnat. Moving as quietly as her leather shoes would take her, Feeyah left the common room and went back to the dormitory where the unmarried brownie women lived —herself included.

The room was empty, the other women still at their chores, but soon the half-dozen of them would be back, filling the air with their chatter and questions. Questions she hardly knew how to answer.

With a shaky sigh, she sat upon the coarse woolen blanket covering her bed.

"Well, then." Biddy strode into the room and regarded Feeyah. "Seems as though you've come out of this well enough, my girl. Now, let's see to that wrist of yours."

FOR SEVEN HAPPY YEARS, Feeyah was playmate and confidante to young Ian as he grew from a sweet boy to a gangly tree of a lad. His parents laughed and shook their heads whenever he played with his "imaginary friend," and Feeyah was very careful to never let them catch a glimpse of her.

She had, at last, gained some wisdom in the brownie ways. She'd gained a husband as well, and two sweet young bairns that filled their home with mischief and laughter.

Still, when the day came that she stood at Ian's bedside and he could no longer see her, sorrow opened a small, permanent hole in the corner of her heart.

Slowly, she pulled a worn kerchief from her pocket and dabbed at her eyes. The linen soaked up her tears, darkening the tiny square of cloth.

Feeyah held it a moment, then with a single shake and muttered word, dispelled the brownie magic she had laid upon it. The kerchief billowed out, one more its original size. Carefully, she laid it on the end of Ian's bed. A full-sized bed it was now, no longer the small truckle he'd used to sleep in.

"Farewell," Feeyah said, in a voice he could not hear. "May many fine adventures await you, my strong and merry lad."

"Hey," he said, snatching the kerchief up. Even though Feeyah stood less than a handspan away, he did not see her. Would never see her again. "Where'd this old thing come from?"

He rubbed at Feeyah's tearstains with his thumb, then shrugged and shoved the kerchief in his pocket. Whistling, he rose and strode from the cottage into the bright sunshine of a summer's morn.

Feeyah watched him go. She swallowed her sorrow—but already something was taking its place. A need, a calling lodged deep in the core of her.

It seemed her reprieve from cleaning was finally at an end.

With a sigh, she turned and pulled his bedcovers straight. Heavy of heart, light of spirit, she conjured up her old broom and began to sweep.

∾

# MUSIC'S PRICE

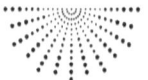

SOMETIMES, when Jeremy Cahill practiced the cello, he'd glimpse *things* out of the corner of his eye. Oddly-joined creatures scuttling along the dingy baseboard of their midtown Manhattan apartment, shimmers of brightness in the dark hallway where no stray sunbeam ever reached.

He was eight the first time he saw them, and tried to tell Ma, but she'd laughed and tousled his hair.

"Ah, Jemmy, you have the Irish gift of blarney. Your gran would be proud. Now, put the instrument away and help me with supper."

As his skill on the cello grew, the uncanny visitors came more frequently. Twig-jointed creatures gathered like bare branches outside the window to listen, slight maidens in gossamer-pale gowns danced like moonbeams—one moment shadow, the next a flicker of light. No one else could see them, and the instant he stopped playing, they vanished.

The creatures were uncanny, but not frightening. Until the day a hollow-eyed banshee appeared, dipping a boy's clothes in the sudden, blood-red stream cutting through his bedroom.

The next morning, his cousin was hit by a car while riding his bike to school, and died instantly. After that, Jeremy refused to practice, refused to even take his cello out of the case, a case that now resembled a coffin.

His dad called him into the living room after a month of sullen non-practicing.

"All the money we've spent over the years, for nothing?" Dad's face reddened, anger thickening his brogue.

He paced around his tan recliner, yelling about the cost, the waste, the brilliance that already had a teacher from the renowned Juilliard School of Music giving Jeremy twice-a-month special lessons.

"Well?" he finally demanded, meaty arms crossed. "Give me one reason."

Jeremy stared at the green carpeting, sick guilt sticking in his throat. He shook his head.

"Christ." Dad let out a beer-scented gust of breath. "Get your coat, lad. Maybe your gran can make some sense of you. Don't come home until she does. And you're ready to practice the damned cello again."

It was a slow bus ride uptown. Jeremy stared out the sleet-spattered windows the whole time, ignoring the other passengers.

When he showed up at her door, Gran took one look at Jeremy's face and sat him down at her kitchen table. She poured him out a cup of strong black tea, using the good china with the gold rim. Without a word, she pushed the sugar and milk over, then waited quietly while he drank. It was the taste of safety.

Surrounded by the yellow warmth of her kitchen, the misery inside him finally uncoiled. He was thirteen, too old to cry, but he set his forehead on the table and wept like a little kid. The lace tablecloth pressed uncomfortably into his skin, but that was nothing compared to the shattering of his heart.

"There, there, *mo chroí*," Gran said, rubbing his hunched-over shoulders. "Tell me."

Her steel-grey hair was crimped in perfect waves, her dress—he'd never seen her in pants—printed with saggy blue flowers. She clomped around the kitchen in her thick black shoes, fixing a plate of sandwiches.

In between blowing his nose, and more tea, and devouring the sandwiches slathered with butter, he told her.

She nodded wisely. "Tis the Sight, love. A rare gift, to be able to see the fair folk."

"I don't want it." He was weird enough, being the musical genius kid, but this—just, no. "I can't play Gran. It's not fair. I can't play ever again unless it goes away."

His voice cracked on the words. Music was the air he breathed—the thing that carried him through the bitter halls of Taft Junior High, the shell protecting his soft, inner core. He couldn't *not* play. But he couldn't bear what the music brought.

Gran studied him, her thin lips pursed. "Well now. Bide here a moment."

She stumped into the parlor, and he heard her opening drawers and rustling around. When she returned, she laid an odd assortment on the table in front of him: a small square of linen, a spool of red thread, a four-leaf clover leached to gray from decades of being pressed in her Bible, and a hard, dry berry the color of old blood.

Jeremy stared at the objects, trying to guess their use. They made no pattern he could see, especially when his grandmother added the tin of oatmeal and her prized crystal salt cellar.

"Um, Gran. What are you doing?"

It looked like a crazy recipe—one he had no intention of tasting. She sat across from him, the spindle-backed chair creaking when she leaned forward.

"You need a charm, my lad. A ward to banish the fair folk, to keep your own heart from breaking. I see how it is with you. Open this." She handed him the smooth yellow tin.

He pried the top off, and she took a pinch of oats and dropped them in the center of the linen square.

"Wait, what? Is this some kind of magic spell or something?" Jeremy frowned, feeling his lips squeeze together. "That's crazy."

Gran gave him a stern look. "This, from the boy that sees the fair folk. Come now, Jemmy. Give me the rowan berry."

That must be the dried bead of fruit. One by one he handed his grandmother each item she requested. She carefully placed them on the cloth, humming softly. At the end, she picked up her salt cellar and gave the entire concoction a thorough salting. Grains of salt drifted over the table like snow.

"Thread the needle, there's a good lad. Double-strung." She folded the edges of the linen square together.

Jeremy licked the end of the thread and managed to get it through the eye on the second try. Gran nodded at him and deftly began sewing precise red stitches against the white cloth, making a neat little packet. Her humming turned to words, the crush and wash of Gaelic like waves on a distant island shore, soughing and sighing up against stone.

When she finished, she tied a firm knot at the end and snipped the thread with a small pair of scissors.

"Some string now," she said. "Fetch it from the top drawer, there."

Jeremy pulled the drawer open and studied the jumble inside. The catchall, the one place in Gran's kitchen that wasn't perfectly tidy and neat. A long curl of one of his old cello strings sprung up to tangle his fingers. Boy, Gran sure kept some useless bits around.

"Bring that," she said.

"My old *D*? What for?"

"It's string, isn't it?" She gave him a level look.

No point in arguing, though technically it was made of nylon and steel, not string at all. Still, he wouldn't argue with Gran—not when she put the eye on him like that. He handed the string to her and she affixed the linen packet halfway down with loops of red thread. Murmuring in Gaelic again, she took the needle and stabbed her index finger.

"Gran!"

"Hush now, *acushla*." A fat, bright drop of blood fell to the center of the linen, spread and wicked into the cloth, a crimson starburst. She held up the weird-looking necklace, the ends of the *D* string corkscrewing around her fingers. "Your charm of safekeeping. Wear it when you play, and the fair folk will stay their distance."

He took it, weighing it in his palm. The doubt must have shown on his face, because she cupped her wrinkled hands around his.

"I promise," she said.

"Okay." He tucked the charm in his pocket. "Thanks, Gran. I should go home."

She firmed her lips. "Believe."

"I will."

He'd try, anyway. And she was right; he'd seen way more strange things than he could explain. Maybe the charm would help save him. Jeremy kissed her dry, rose-scented cheek, and, hope catching in his throat, caught the bus back midtown.

When he got home, he didn't say anything to his dad, just got his cello out, tuned it up, and started practicing.

Gran's charm worked. At least, it did for the next seven years.

INSIDE THE CHURCH, the dimly-lit air swirled with candle smoke and incense. After the priest finished saying the words he nodded to where Jeremy sat, to the left of Gran's black coffin. Jeremy pulled his cello back against his body, the wood gleaming like rich toffee. The long scratch marring the finish was hidden by his black trouser leg—a small mercy in a day filled with too much misery.

He glanced at his parents sitting in the front pew, their hands tightly woven together. Dad was thinner now, his skin grayish from the chemo. He'd removed his ever-present cap, and the bare skin of his scalp shone with perspiration. Beside him, Jeremy's mother looked smaller, the strain of the last year etched on her face in new lines.

The priest cleared his throat, and Jeremy began to play. He started with one of Gran's favorites, *Si Bheag, Si Mhor*, the notes rising up to flutter like moths against the stained glass.

On the daylit side of the windows, he glimpsed twiggy

creatures crouching. A distant siren sped through the city streets, and he heard the echo of his name in its high wailing.

No. Oh no.

The fair folk had returned. They couldn't enter the church, but he felt them outside. Waiting.

Fear thick in his throat, Jeremy kept playing. He'd promised Gran he'd play at her funeral.

"Not just the sad tunes, Jemmy," she'd told him, her fingers frail in his grasp, her skin yellow against the too-white hospital pillows. "You must remember the good, as well. Play a reel for me. The angels will like that."

She'd looked at him, the echo of her old self brightening in her eyes.

*Don't go, Gran.* Grief had crushed his breath, but he'd managed a smile for her.

"I will," he said.

But he'd never expected the cost. As the music spooled out from under his fingers, the charm that had held the fair folk at bay for so long faltered, its power fading. Still, he played.

Jeremy's dad frowned, his way of holding back tears, and Jeremy slid into a different tune, *The Broken Pledge*, an old reel in a minor key. For Gran's memory, for the scrap of linen and string tucked beneath his shirt—useless now.

He played the tune three times through, then lifted his bow from the strings, the cello still vibrating against his knees.

Nobody applauded—they wouldn't at a funeral—but he could see how the power of the music touched them. His mother blew her nose discreetly into her linen kerchief. The priest gave a final blessing, and freed the congregation. The burial was later that afternoon.

Jeremy waited for the church to empty, fear and sorrow curdling in his stomach. He didn't want to set foot outside those consecrated walls. Didn't want to say goodbye to Gran, and the magic that had protected him for so long.

"Lovely playing," his mother said, clutching her handkerchief. "I'm so sorry about…. Well. Your gran would be proud."

His dad gripped his shoulder, with a hand that still had some strength to it.

"Well done," he said, a gruff edge in his voice—pride and guilt tangled together.

It wasn't Dad's fault he'd gotten sick and the money had run out like water through a sieve. The scholarship Jeremy got from Juilliard wasn't enough to bridge the sudden, yawning chasm in his family's finances. The only option was to drop out of music school. They called it a "leave of absence," but Jeremy knew he wouldn't be back. Not unless things changed drastically—which wasn't going to happen.

The back of his neck tightened as he trailed his parents out of the church. He couldn't see the fair folk, but he sensed their presence. Watching him.

When Gran was buried and the last words said, Jeremy took the subway back to his apartment. He stuck his cello case in the corner, facing away from him. There was no reason to play—no teachers demanding concertos, no quartets depending on him—and every reason not to.

What if, the next time he played, the banshee came again, warning of his dad's imminent death? No. He wouldn't bear that guilt. To keep the fair folk at bay, he'd stop playing, though his soul might bleed dry from it.

Jeremy ignored his cello for three weeks, spent his days handing in job applications everywhere. But apparently a Juilliard drop-out wasn't even qualified to wash dishes at the deli down the street. The smell of their pastrami sandwiches made his mouth water—he'd been living on ramen and canned peaches for a week—but he couldn't afford anything more. He left, the doorbell jangling behind him. The winter wind slapped his cheeks, but colder still was the knowledge he'd run out of choices.

Pulling his wool pea coat tight, Jeremy trudged back to his unheated apartment. The tiny studio would no longer be his if he didn't come up with rent within the next three days.

He could sell his cello—but the thought made his stomach churn. No. Gran had helped pay for it. Besides, he couldn't get what the instrument was worth on such short notice, and he refused to pawn it.

Hands cold, trying not to dwell on what he was doing, he slung his cello over his shoulder and headed to the West Avenue subway station.

After he'd left school, he'd made a decent enough living— all right, a scraping-by—playing for tips in the subway. He'd found a perfect corner to busk in; close enough to the heater vents so his fingers didn't stiffen from the cold, and enough out of the way that nobody tripped over his cello as they rushed by.

The station was grimed and oily, the tiled walls smeared with handprints, the concrete saturated with acres of ground-in dirt. Bright fluorescent lights cast jagged shadows over the station sign; WEST AVENUE printed in stark black letters.

A hollow wind whooshed from the train tunnel, stirring the discarded gum wrappers and paper cups that had collected in Jeremy's corner. At least nobody had taken the spot. He scooted the trash out of the way with the side of his shoe, then set up his folding stool and unpacked his cello. The battered fedora on his head had a five-dollar bill glued inside. He'd almost ripped it out to buy that pastrami sandwich, but seed-money was crucial—a cue that people should throw real money into his hat, not just dimes and pennies.

He tethered the fedora to his shoelace with a strand of fishing line. When he'd first started busking, he'd learned the hard way how impossible it was to chase a thief while carrying a naked cello. He'd lost nearly thirty bucks that day. Even worse, he'd put a long, painful scrape down his cello's side.

The rumble of the approaching train set his strings to vibrating.

Jeremy took a deep breath and tuned up. Nothing happened, and the tight knot under his ribs eased. Maybe Gran's funeral service had been a fluke. Maybe he was still safe. He lifted one hand to his chest and pressed the charm through the cloth of his t-shirt; the stained linen still strung on a tarnished $D$ around his neck.

With a screech, the train pulled to a stop and the doors hissed open. He pulled his bow across the strings, letting the sweet precision of a Bach sonata soar into the echoing space before it filled up with the clack of shoes, the blur of conversation.

The crowd thickened, streaming past. He'd gotten there just before the commuter hour, the best time to busk. Jeremy didn't openly look at his hat. Another lesson learned. Even though money was the whole point, it was bad form for the performer to pay attention to his take, at least where people could see. They preferred the illusion that musicians played only for love.

Still, watching from the corner of his eye, it looked like *nothing* was going into his hat. No bright flash of coins, no flutter of bills. He switched to a faster movement of the Bach.

When the last passengers trailed past, Jeremy pulled the hat over. It held the three quarters and five-spot he'd salted the hat with—and nothing else. Not even a dime.

"Oh, come on," he said to the empty station.

He'd always gotten *something* when he played—a few bucks at least, some pennies. This wasn't just unfair, it was wrong in a way that set his teeth on edge.

For the next wave of commuters, he played Brahms, then Saint-Saens. Nothing.

Anger warmed him through.

"I know what you're doing," he said to the shadows lurking at the edge of the tunnel.

He almost, almost, packed up his cello. But he couldn't leave the station with pockets as empty as he'd come in.

The train whooshed up, disgorging people. Jeremy played Bartok, Bloch, the most modern pieces he knew. His hat stayed empty. Rush hour was almost over, and his chance of making any worthwhile money slipping away.

Damn them.

He was finally there, playing, and it wasn't enough.

Fingers tight around his bow, Jeremy waited until the crowd was upon him. Then he launched into Gran's favorite jig; *The Lark in the Morning.*

Beyond the emptying platform, the shadows crept closer on spindle-shanks and goblin feet. He swallowed, hard, and kept playing. Eyes watched him from the edges. Things moved where they shouldn't.

But his hat filled with uncanny speed.

As the station emptied, Jeremy stilled his cello strings. He pulled his hat over, and caught his breath. Money filled the battered fedora. Carefully smoothing each bill, he counted his take. Forty-two dollars and seventy-three cents.

So, that's how it was going to be. Play the old tunes, or end up homeless on the bitter winter streets.

"Fine," he said, though it was so far from fine he wanted to weep.

One more wave of commuters left. If he was going to do this, he'd do it all the way. Just once.

This time he played from his heart, the way he hadn't let himself before. The sweet notes unfurled from beneath his fingers, the body of his cello resonating against his chest as he played one of his best tunes; *Farewell to Ireland*. The crowd flowed past, fingers drumming in time against legs, against briefcases. One lady held her phone out toward him for a moment before moving on. Though nobody lingered—they almost never did—it took longer than usual for the station to clear.

When the last set of heels disappeared up the stairs, Jeremy looked in his hat. Blinked, heartbeat pounding in his throat. The fedora was overflowing with bills, and not just singles.

"Damn," he breathed.

He counted the money out into a neat stack. One-hundred-sixty-five dollars and twenty-two cents. Unbelievable.

An unearthly giggle from the far platform, the glitter of a fey eye—it was past time for him to leave. Shivering, Jeremy shoved the money in his pocket and jammed his fedora on his head.

He closed his cello case, snicking the latches shut. The

sound echoed, louder than it should, and a chill clutched the back of his neck. Something was watching from deep in the subway tunnel. A murmur built, like the sound of untamed waves. Keeping his gaze averted, Jeremy shouldered his cello and dashed up the stairs into the neon-broken night above.

But the next afternoon he reluctantly hauled his cello back to the grubby corner of the West Avenue Station. He was still short on the rent, though another few hours' playing should do it. Then he could stop; for good.

What if he didn't stop?

He tried to push the thought to the back of his mind, but it kept surfacing. The possibilities froze him with terror, burned him with hope.

If he played another day or two, gritted his teeth and tried not to see the creatures the music brought, he could make enough to help with Dad's next treatment. The fair folk already haunted his nightmares, after all. He could bear it a little longer.

Maybe.

Jeremy rosined his bow, the faint scent of old sap tickling his nose as he pulled the horsehair back and forth across the dark rectangle of rosin. Even before he started playing, he glimpsed them lurking in the shadows— misshapen bodies and legs that bent the wrong way, the starlit sheen of wings.

"I don't believe in you," he told them. The lie grated in his throat.

He waited to play until the trains disgorged their passengers, and stopped his music the instant the last person passed. Then began again at the next wave of commuters. Jaw tight, he played the hardest tunes he knew: complex five part slip-jigs, rambunctious reels pulsing in duple-beat rhythms, polkas that ratcheted his bow from string to string.

The fair folk watched. And listened. And came closer, their numbers growing.

Tens, twenties poured into his hat. Even a fifty, from a man who wore a suit worth ten times that amount. Jeremy didn't feel too guilty. People only put in what they could spare. A single bill, multiplied by a few hundred, added up.

He went home with over a thousand dollars, aching shoulders—and an unearthly escort. A chime of fey laughter in a dark alleyway, something flitting between parked cars, a black dog trotting down the sidewalk half a block behind, tongue lolling.

Jeremy whirled. "Leave me alone!"

Just another crazy yelling on the Manhattan streets. Nobody even looked his way.

Bitter knowledge sifted through his body, speeding his heart, drying his mouth. In all the old stories Gran had told him, there was no escape from the fair folk.

Not when they wanted you.

THE NEXT DAY, Jeremy paused at the top of the West Avenue Station stairs. Cello case straps digging into his shoulders, he tilted his face up to the wan winter sun, trying to memorize the feeling of sunlight against his skin.

Chill fingers combed through his hair, icy wind-borne maidens invisible to the passers-by on the street. Creatures leaned out from the bare-twigged bushes to clutch at his jeans with long, crooked nails.

*Jemmy Cahill.* The syllables of his name in the squeal of brakes, the cries of children, the sudden thrum of pigeon wings as a flock arose from the stained sidewalk.

Whether he returned to the light of the human world, or disappeared forever into the shadows, this had to end.

With a deep breath, Jeremy headed down into the closed-in dimness of the station. The air changed as he descended. The haze of oil and exhaust stayed up on the streets, but a different smell wound up from the platform below—something wild, tinged with the salt of the sea.

He didn't look at the metal rails of the tracks, tried not to think about the darkness they disappeared into.

That morning, he'd woken up knowing what he had to play. The oldest tunes, the eerie modal ones that wept and sang through his cello. The ones that spoke of loss and heartbreak and magics disappearing forever from the world.

He walked past his corner and went right up to the edge of the platform. Quickly, he unfolded his stool, unpacked his cello, and began. An ancient, nameless air to start, the notes vibrating low, soaring up into the high part like a woman weeping. When that tune ended, he moved into a dark, twisty jig called *The Orphan.*

The air in the station stilled. The light shifted, shading to amber. Jeremy looked up at the station sign and his fingers trembled, nearly dropping his bow. Instead of WEST AVENUE the sign now read WIDDERSHINS.

He finished the tune, the last note fading away into a world that was no longer his own.

Gran would tell him to have courage. Jeremy stood, his cello balanced beside him on the slender silver endpin, the embodiment of all his hopes. All his fears. He didn't want to be sitting down when he faced whatever was coming.

A sound issued from the dark tunnel, a high keening that had nothing to do with machinery. Jeremy's pulse throbbed queasily at the back of his throat. Whispering a desperate, useless Hail Mary, he squeezed his eyes closed.

When he opened them again, a train sat at the platform. He hadn't heard it arrive. It resembled the usual A-line cars—white and red, and filled with passengers—but the differences were enough to make his breath tighten in narrowing circles of fear.

He clutched the neck of his cello as if it was the only solid thing in the universe. Oh, he'd set things in motion he had no idea how to end. All he knew was that the fair folk must be faced, or they would drive him to madness.

The train doors silently opened, and the riders stepped out.

Pale maidens with moth-tangled hair, gowned in cobwebs. Twig-jointed creatures with staring eyes. Goblins wearing caps of blood. Sharp-fanged, sinuous hounds. The hollow-eyed banshee. The shambling bog horse.

All the lovely, horrible creatures he had tried not to see his whole life.

And behind them...

Behind them strode a figure clad in midnight. A band of silver encircled his moon-pale hair, and his face was sharp-planed and merciless. Nothing human shone in those starlit eyes.

A shudder crimped Jeremy's spine, and he looked away, wishing he'd brought something—an iron cross, even a handful of salt—to defend himself.

Gran had whispered stories to him once, of the Sidhe lords and ladies gone far to the west, taking their magic with them. The knowledge of what he now faced lodged deep in Jeremy's lungs. He breathed through the stabbing truth of it.

"Jemmy Cahill," the elf-lord said, his voice like frost and famine. "Do you think you can deny us the taste of your music for seven long years without paying a price?"

Swallowing back the sharp tang of fear, Jeremy dug in his pocket and brought out the roll of bills he'd earned busking in the station.

"Here."

The lord laughed, a sound like metal scraping bone. "What use have I for such? You must offer better coin than that."

What else did he have to give? Fingers numb, Jeremy reached beneath his shirt and pulled out Gran's charm. He tugged it from his neck and held it out.

One of the twiggy creatures crept over and snatched it from his hand, and Jeremy flinched back. The watching fair folk laughed, their voices chiming and barking, a cacophony echoed back from the curved ceiling overhead.

The creature delivered the charm to his liege, and the elf-lord held it up, a pathetic scrap of soiled linen and tarnished string.

"A spent ward?" The lord's voice was hollow with fey mirth. "This counts for less than nothing."

He tossed it into the air. A bright flash, the afterimage seared on the inside of Jeremy's eyelids, and Gran's charm was gone.

"Hey! That wasn't fair." Anger made Jeremy straighten, though he couldn't quite look upon the beautiful, terrible face of the elf-lord.

"Do not speak to us of fairness. Is it fair to deny the Sight that runs through your blood? Is it fair to bind your music so tightly it withers to nothing, when we starve to hear it?" At his words, the watching fair folk nodded and murmured. "Your time has run, mortal child. Choose your path."

Jeremy held his cello in front of him like a shield. For a stark moment he considered setting the instrument down and walking away.

Far away, to a place where music didn't matter. Where his soul could shrink and shrivel into normalcy. Where the stuff of nightmares didn't stalk through the shadows of the subway tunnels, or whisper from the corners of alleyways.

The stuff of nightmares.

And dreams. Dark and light entwined, like the night-brilliant lord standing before him, and all his dancing, dreadful court.

Jeremy took a shuddering breath flavored with the scent of the sea. Gran would have wanted him to choose the magic that ran in their shared blood. This was his heritage, his very soul. Clamping his fingers hard around his cello, he met the elf-lord's fathomless gaze.

"I will play for you," Jeremy said. "I will give you my music. Just—don't kill me."

He couldn't simply disappear on his parents. It would break them beyond repair.

Something shivered over the assembled fair folk, triumph and avarice mixed together in the sweet, feral eyes turned upon him.

The lord laughed, his voice resonant with victory. "We have no intentions of ending your mortal life."

Jeremy let out a ragged sigh of relief, but the lord was not finished speaking.

"But when next the moon is full," he said, a fierce light in his eldritch eyes, "you will come join us. Seven years you owe us, mortal, and seven years you shall remain as a bard within our courts. We shall come for you in a fortnight. Be ready."

Seven years? A chill swept over him. Dad could be dead by then, Mom wasted away by grief. His few friends would forget him, and his career at Juilliard would be completely finished.

Yet the choice had already been made. Gran had always said beware the bargains of the fair folk.

Despite the terror flickering through his veins, something else stirred—a wild and secret joy. He had his music back, and would see magic beyond mortal ken. It was almost worth the price.

The elf-lord turned to leave, and Jeremy lifted his hand.

"Wait!" he cried. "One more thing."

The lord narrowed his bright eyes. "Our business here is done."

"My dad is sick." Jeremy thought furiously. "I'd only play melancholy tunes for you, if I knew he was dying and me not by his side. Can you save him?"

The lord did not reply for a long moment, and Jeremy's heart beat desperately. Please. Please.

"We cannot cure him," the elf-lord said. "But we will ensure he lives until you return to the human world."

It was enough. Jeremy bowed his head.

When he looked up again, the fair folk were gone. Cold air pressed his skin, then heat. Sound returned—the screech of train brakes nearly deafening in the brightly-lit station. He swayed, the taste of starlight and ashes on his tongue.

The crowd, the blessedly human crowd, surged out of the train and headed for the stairs. They brushed past Jeremy, heads bent to screens and phones, heedless.

"You okay, man?" A guy about his age paused and caught his elbow. "You might want to get your instrument out of the way."

Blinking hard, Jeremy scooted back into the shelter of his corner. He settled on his stool, then toed his upside-down fedora a few inches out. Glancing down at his cello, he caught his breath at the smooth, unmarred surface.

Not everything could be mended by magic, but that wouldn't stop him from trying.

Setting his bow on the strings, he began to play.

# THE FIRST ADVENTURE

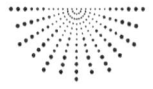

## A FEYLAND PREQUEL

JENNET CARTER SNEAKED into the computer room, her heart beating too loudly in the stillness. She closed the door, holding her breath until the lock clicked solidly home. It was silly, being so nervous in her own house, but still. She didn't want any of the staff walking in on her while she hacked her dad's new sim equipment.

She padded across the plush carpeting to the prototype version of the FullD system, and ran her hand over the smooth curve of the sim helmet. The room lights reflected off the visor like miniature stars.

The most immersive gaming equipment ever designed was *here*, in their house—had been for two weeks—and so far all she'd been allowed to do was run around on grids and jump off blocky gray squares. Her dad wasn't the best player, despite being lead project manager on the FullD, so he let Jennet gear up while he took notes for the programmers. It was kind of fun, in a boring way. At least she got a chance to learn how to use the sim gear.

Then, last night, she'd noticed a new icon as she logged on; an *F* made of scrolled golden flame.

When she asked Dad about it, he'd made some weak excuse and hustled her off the system. Luckily, she knew his password. He hadn't changed it in three years. She should say something. But then, how would she be able to access the stuff he didn't want her to see?

Jennet hit the power button and slid into the sim chair, cushioned in fresh-smelling black faux leather. She donned the helmet, then pulled on the gaming gloves. The embedded LEDs winked at her as the system powered up, the sensor nodes on the gloves glinting like precious jewels: amethysts, rubies, emeralds.

At the loading interface, she lifted her finger and selected the new, flame-colored icon.

Haunting, mysterious music played through the helmet, and anticipation tingled through her. What was Dad hiding? What amazing new game was VirtuMax developing to go with their new technology?

Words appeared across the black background of the visor:

*Feyland: A VirtuMax Production*

*Alpha 1.1.923*

**WELCOME TO FEYLAND**

The letters glowed golden, then deepened to crimson as flames flickered along the sides. The music rose, and the words whirled up into a flurry of leaves the color of ashes. Behind them... Jennet blinked, a chill running through her. Was that a pair of eyes, gleaming from the shadows?

If the programmers were trying to create an eerie opening, they'd definitely succeeded.

The shivery feeling lingered, even as the standard charac-

ter-creation interface popped up. She scanned the limited
options: Knight, Spellcaster, or Bard. It didn't take long to
read the descriptions and make her decision. She always liked
being a magic-user in other games, so it was a no-brainer to
choose Spellcaster.

Judging by the lack of options in the character menu, this
was a very rough draft of the game. Jennet chose blue eyes
and blonde hair—her own coloring. Her new character wore
long blue robes and carried a magical-looking staff with a
glowing crystal set in the end. She hoped she wouldn't end up
running her avatar through more featureless gray landscapes
—that would be a serious disappointment.

*Enter game?*

She tipped her thumb up, the universal glove command
for yes.

Dizzying golden light enveloped her senses, and she swallowed. Whatever the programmers were experimenting with,
it made her feel queasy. She wished could share her reactions
and feedback with Dad. But she couldn't tell him she was
using the prototype equipment without his permission.

For once, she was glad he was such a workaholic. As long
as she logged off in time, he'd never know she'd been
accessing Feyland.

The golden light cleared, and Jennet found her avatar
standing in a grassy clearing surrounded by white-barked
trees. She stood in the exact center of a ring of pale mushrooms that glowed like the moon. The sunlit grass under her
feet was springy and soft, and she swore she could feel the
wind against her face.

Wow. The developers had done a ton of work with the
immersion software. This was nothing like the primary

simulations Dad had her running around in. This world felt *real*. A faint, spicy scent tickled her nose—the smell of herbs and warm grasses. Jennet breathed in deeply, and smiled.

A breeze riffled the leaves, their undersides flashing silver, and birdsong lilted through the air. On the far side of the clearing, a fern-draped path beckoned. Taking a firm grip on her staff, Jennet jumped over the circle of mushrooms and started forward in search of adventure.

THE DARK QUEEN reclined on her throne of tangled branches, stars snared in her midnight hair. Her dress was made of moonlight and shadows. Around her the denizens of the Dark Court thronged, fey eyes glittering. Twig-limbed creatures crouched beside the throne, flanked by gossamer-winged maidens. Beneath the dark trees, hounds with glowing red eyes paced back and forth, held in check only by their antler-helmed master.

A goblin approached the throne. Trembling, he bowed and swept off his blood-red cap, keeping his gaze averted from the terrible beauty of his ruler.

"What news?" the queen asked, in a voice colder than winter ice.

The goblin bowed even lower. "A human presence has been sensed at the edge of the Realm."

The Dark Queen stood, her eyes deep as night-dark pools. Her long, pale fingers curled eagerly at her sides.

"Another human? Tell me everything."

"My queen—I know little." The goblin shivered, clearly

hoping his lack of knowledge would not prove his death. "It is a female, younger than the man…."

He hesitated. The queen did not take kindly to reminders of her failure.

The Dark Queen slashed the air with her hand. "Go on."

"A mortal girl. She is being watched."

"A young one." The queen smiled, a sharp, dreadful expression on her inhuman face. "Bring her to me, but carefully. We will make no mistakes with this one."

"Aye, my lady."

On shaking limbs, the goblin scuttled away. He did not dare turn his back on the Dark Queen, or the avid, feral members of her court. As a redcap goblin, he was vicious—but one redcap alone was no match for the creatures under her command.

At last, reaching the edge of her court, he turned and fled; past the eerie violet-hued bonfire where figures capered around the flames, past the high, keening laughter of a banshee, past the forbiddingly still figure of the Huntsman, his antlered head silhouetted against the late sky.

JENNET FOLLOWED the mossy path through the white-barked trees. Sunlight sifted in golden shafts between the trunks, and yellow-winged butterflies danced against the deeper shadows of the woods. The oak of her mage staff was smooth and solid under her palm.

This was prime. By *far* the best sim experience she'd ever had. VirtuMax had done an amazing job with their new tech.

It was hard to believe she was in a prototype game, the interface felt so smooth.

Something rustled in the bushes beside the path, and she whirled, her breath catching.

"Who's there?"

No reply. She stood for a long moment, scanning the underbrush, but saw nothing. Warily, Jennet started down the path again. Just because she was in the beginning level of the game didn't mean she was safe. Monsters and creatures could spring out to attack her at any moment. That's how these fantasy-type games went.

Although usually a character picked up a quest first, instead of wandering around in the woods, waiting to be attacked. Clearly Feyland was still in the rudimentary storyline phase. She had nothing to go on, beyond exploring the world and hoping to figure things out. No prompts, no cues, no text explaining what her game objectives were.

But as long as the world was so amazing, she didn't care. The game developers would give her something to do soon enough.

The trees thinned, showing glimpses of emerald meadows and azure sky beyond. Jennet stepped out of the trees, and smiled at the view. Rolling hills spread out before her, spangled with white blossoms. Nestled in a nearby hollow stood a cozy-looking cottage, full-on fairytale with its whitewashed, half-timbered walls and diamond-paned windows. Red flowers spilled from the window boxes.

The path she stood on led directly to the front step.

A brown, squat creature sat there, watching her. Her first quest-giver? Or an enemy? There was nothing about it to give her any indication—no green friendly icon over its head, or red shield that would signal aggression. In most sim games, NPCs, Non-Player-Characters, were marked so that players knew how to interact. Obviously, the programmers had a bit more work to do on the game.

Pressing her lips together in concentration, Jennet reviewed her Spellcaster's arsenal. Fireball, Wall of Flame, and Arcane Blast. All three spells seemed strong enough to take down an enemy, though Wall of Flame had a ten second cooldown that made it less useful. Still, it seemed a decent enough assortment to work with.

Jennet strode down the path toward the cottage. As she approached, the figure on the doorstep looked up at her. He was a hideous creature.

His dark eyes and thin lips were overshadowed by his enormous, jutting cliff of a nose. The only things larger than his nose were his ears, great ugly flaps of skin on either side of his head. He was covered in a pelt of coarse brown hair, his only clothing a tattered cloth tied about his waist.

He didn't seem primed to attack, so Jennet stepped closer, wrinkling her nose at the smell of moldy earth and old wood-smoke. She halted a few feet from the stoop, waiting, but the creature only regarded her from its murky brown eyes.

"Hello?" she said at last.

"Greetings." His voice sounded like stirred gravel. "Did you bring me milk?"

She glanced around. Was there supposed to be a store nearby? Had she missed a step somewhere?

He folded his spindly arms. "I want milk."

"Okay."

If this was the first quest, it was a strange one. She wished she could give the developers some advice.

Clearly she wasn't going to get anywhere with the weird little creature until she'd brought him milk. Whatever. Jennet walked around the cottage, looking for clues, and when she got back to the front step, the creature was holding a wooden bowl cradled between his knobbly fingers.

"Slow-witted mortal," he said, holding out the bowl. "Fill this with milk from the black cow over yonder hill."

Jennet took it, careful not to touch the creature. Something about him was just too odd for comfort. Bowl tucked under her arm, she headed for the rise behind the cottage. The wind tugged a strand of her hair free, and she pushed it behind her ear. She could almost feel the warm sunshine, like a hand upon her shoulder.

At the top of the hill she took a moment to appreciate the view. The grassy hills, green-gold in the sunlight, rolled away before her. A small valley lay below, the silvery glint of a stream at the bottom edged by graceful cottonwoods. Farther out, a darker line of trees stood. Pines, maybe. Behind them, the blue shadows of mountains rose, jagged against the sky.

The world of Feyland beckoned, a fantastic place to explore. But first, she had to get some milk.

A white fence enclosed a small field below, holding—as the creature had promised—a black cow. She'd never actually milked a cow before, but surely the game designers wouldn't make it too hard.

Of course, she had to catch the cow first. Jennet climbed over the fence. The cow watched her with soft, placid eyes, but every time she got close enough to grasp the red harness it wore, somehow the animal ended up on the other side of the meadow.

She plucked handfuls of grass to entice it, tried sprinting and sneaking, and finally, after ten useless minutes, gave it up.

Fine. Jennet set the bowl down and crossed her arms, deliberately ignoring the animal. What else could she use? There was nothing in her in-game inventory, and somehow she didn't think blasting the cow with a Fireball would help. The creature had asked for milk, not rare steak.

There was some quote… something about music soothing the savage beast. Could that be the answer? And was it even possible to catch a cow with music?

She had to at least try, no matter how farfetched the notion. Leaning back against the white fence, she hummed a snatch of song they were working on in youth choir—*Ca' the Yowes*.

To her surprise, the game picked up the song and amplified it. Jennet straightened. She started singing for real, pulling the air deep into her lungs and letting out a strand of melody that felt almost tangible.

*Ca' the yowes to the knowes,*
*Ca' them where the heather grows,*
*Ca' them where the burnie rowes,*
*My bonnie dearie.*

The cow lifted its head and took a step forward. Jennet imagined the song surrounding the black cow, looping around its broad neck and leading it forward. The animal took another step toward her, then another. *It was working!* Keeping her breath steady, Jennet kept singing, drawing the cow closer and closer. At the last verse, she grasped the supple red leather of its harness with a burst of triumph.

The cow snorted when the song ended, but didn't seem too unhappy to be caught. Jennet tied the cow to the fence rail and picked up the bowl. Giving a doubtful glance at the udder, she squatted down.

Was she actually supposed to grab the gross pink flesh? What if she pulled too hard, and the cow kicked her? Those hooves looked sharp.

She could do this. Really.

Jennet slid the bowl under the udder and grabbed one of the teats. It was warm to her touch, and she tried not to shudder. Pull and squeeze, right? She tugged, and thankfully, a white stream shot out, straight into the bowl.

A dozen more pulls, and the bowl was nearly full. Jennet carefully set it beyond the fence, then untied the cow.

"Thank you," she said, and turned it loose.

It uttered a low moo and trotted to the far side of the field. A second later it started munching the grass, ignoring her completely.

The smell of warm milk drifted up to tickle her nose. Careful not to spill, she carried the bowl back over the hill and set it in front of the creature who still waited on the step.

"Ah!" he cried with glee.

Picking up the offering, he guzzled the milk in one long swallow. He looked happier when he was finished, his face plumper and not so scowly. Still really ugly, though.

He nodded at her, dark eyes gleaming. "So, mortal. My use-name is Fynnod, and I welcome you to the Realm."

"Thanks. I'm—"

"We will name you Fair Jennet here," he said. "What do you seek?"

He knew her name? That was weird—but then, she *had* logged in under the user name of Jennet. Of course she didn't use her real name when playing actual games, but this was just the pre-beta.

"I seek..."

She paused. What was the goal of Feyland, anyway? The intro storyline was non-existent. Clearly it was a fantasy-type game, but what was the objective?

Fynnod was no help. He sat, still as a stone, and watched her.

"Victory," she finally said in a firm voice.

"Then you shall continue further into the Realm." He nodded, something murky and unpleasant moving through his eyes. "Be brave, Fair Jennet. I will send you to the next circle of Feyland."

He lifted his hand, fingers twisting in a complex pattern. Glowing runes inscribed the air, and Jennet blinked. A moment later, white light swirled around her. The blue sky over her head tipped and shredded away. Jennet gripped her staff tightly, forcing herself to stay calm. It was just a game. It couldn't hurt her, no matter how real it felt.

The light cleared, and she found herself standing in another clearing, the same pale mushrooms encircling her. This time, though, dark pines surrounded her. The sky overhead was the pearly gray of impending dusk, the air heavy with the scent of dust and sap.

So, this was the second level of the game. She frowned. The starting lands were more appealing, with the wide horizon and sunlit hills. She wouldn't have minded spending more time exploring there, but clearly the game had other ideas.

Chiming laughter scattered through the air like glitter, and Jennet glanced up to see silvery balls of light floating through the trees. Squinting, she could make out small, winged figures in the center of each shimmering light. Faeries.

They floated to the edge of the forest and hovered, illuminating the beginning of another path. All right. She had time to do a little more adventuring.

Jennet stepped over the mushroom ring, and followed the glimmering creatures down the path. A thick carpet of pine needles muffled her footsteps. Wisps of gray mist floated through the trees, and she was grateful for the little faeries leading the way. Occasionally one would laugh, like high tinkling bells, and they all would float faster. Jennet picked up her pace until she was running through the silent forest, the shimmering lights bobbing ahead.

The crystal set at the end of her staff glowed, sending a dim bluish glow onto the path. No obstacles blocked her way, no fallen limbs or thorny brambles. Dark violet flowers studded the nearby bushes, pulsing oddly in the light.

At last, the balls of light slowed. When Jennet reached them they floated slowly upward, higher and higher, until they twinkled like stars against the evening sky. Then they winked out.

"Hey," she called. "Come back!"

Even though they'd seemed more like fireflies than sentient beings, she'd been glad of their company. The forest was darker now, the stillness full of menace. Throat suddenly dry, Jennet looked around to see where the faerie creatures had led her.

A dark ruin rose among the trees, a tower, crumbling against the sky. Its empty door gaped blackly. Had something moved in those deep shadows?

Usually she was up for any kind of fight, in-game, but this

just felt creepy. Her heartbeat pounded in her chest, frantically sending the message *go home, go home.*

Too late.

A figure stepped from the doorway; an armored knight clad all in black. The shadows slid away from him, as though his armor were made of an even deeper blackness. His helm completely obscured his face. If he had a face at all.

Jennet raised her staff, her mind scrabbling to recall her spells. She had no doubt *this* was a true enemy.

"Fair Jennet," the figure rasped, lifting a huge sword, "prepare to meet the Black Knight in battle."

Oh damn. Spellcaster against heavily armored fighter. This couldn't end well.

Forcing back her fear, Jennet called up Wall of Flame. Before the knight took another step forward, a sheet of fire roared from her staff and enveloped him.

He bellowed and strode forward, seemingly untouched. Jennet sidled to the right and sent an Arcane Blast at her enemy. A bolt of blue sizzled through the air like lightning, and she took advantage of the distraction to dart for the edge of the tower. Her best bet was to stay out of range of that dangerous sword and try to wear the knight down with magic. If he got close...

Well, she wouldn't let him.

But he was fast. Before she could summon her next spell, he charged her. She danced back as his blade whistled past, far too close. She wasn't ready to die in-game. Not yet. Keeping new characters alive for as long as possible was a point of honor for her.

She called up a Fireball and flung it straight at the knight. Orange-red flame scorched through the air, and he staggered back a pace. Jennet slid further around the tower. Maybe she could make a break for the trees, use them for cover.

Clang! The sword bit into the stones right above her head. She dodged away, blinking grit from her eyes. The knight was fast—too fast. His next attack came before she was ready, his sword slicing across her chest. A burning line scored her shoulder, and she stumbled backward.

And fell through the doorway of the tower, into blackness.

"WHERE IS SHE?" the Dark Queen hissed, in a voice edged with ice. "You were to bring Fair Jennet to me, not cause her to flee!"

A white tracery of frost formed on the Black Knight's chest-piece, proof of his ruler's ire. He bore the cutting cold without complaint.

"I will not fail you again," he said.

The queen crooked her finger, compelling him forward until he stared into her deep, fathomless eyes.

"See that you do not."

She drew a wickedly pointed blackthorn spike from her robes and, faster than thought, plunged it deep into the place his heart should be.

The knight shuddered but held his ground. This was the price of his failure. He would not die from it, though the pain would have sent any other member of the Dark Queen's court screaming to their knees. Instead, he merely bowed his head.

The watching Court laughed: pale maidens gowned in cobwebs, sharp-toothed goblins, hollow-eyed, nameless crea-tures with impossibly twisted limbs, all cackling and gibbering until the noise eclipsed the waning scythe of the moon above.

JENNET PULLED off the sim helmet and shook her head. She felt disoriented and muzzy, as if she'd fallen asleep in the hot sun and cooked her brains. That last fight had not gone well. Good thing the game suddenly glitched out.

She slid her hands from the gloves and stood up. Her shoulder ached—stung, really. Rubbing it, she powered down the FullD system, then checked it over to make sure she'd left no sign of her illicit gaming. Everything looked just the way Dad had left it.

She glanced at the clock and sucked in a breath. It was later than she'd thought. Dad would be home for dinner any minute. Hastily, she left the gaming room, turning the lights off behind her.

Just in time—the front door chimed open and she heard her dad come in, talking to somebody. Had he invited Thomas over?

Sure enough, her father's friend, Thomas Rimer, had joined him after work. Thomas was like an uncle to her. Though she didn't see enough of him, since Dad had gotten him a job with VirtuMax as a lead game designer.

Smiling, she went to the stairs and hung over the railing above the entryway.

"Hey there, Jennet," Thomas said, waving. "Come down. I brought you something."

"You're going to spoil her," Jennet's dad said, but his voice was mild.

She hurried down the stairs, and Thomas handed her the flat package he'd had tucked under his arm.

"What is it?" She lifted it, guessing it was a book. Thomas collected rare old print volumes, though her dad teased him about hoarding dead trees.

"Come, sit," her dad said, playing host.

He shepherded them into the living room, then keyed an order into the house computer; tea for her, wine for Thomas and himself. Their place was old—most of Jennet's friends had voice-activated house networks—but they'd lived in the house for over ten years. Dad bought it after... she swallowed. After her mother took off. She preferred not to remember anything about that time.

No, this was their home, the only one she and Dad needed. Just the two of them. Old tech or not, she liked it that way.

Jennet sat on the soft couch, avoiding the one cushion that pulled people in like a black hole, and carefully peeled back the plain brown paper enclosing her present. As she'd guessed, it was a book—an old one, from the dusty, comforting smell emanating from the pages.

It was bound in green leather, the title worked in raised gold lettering: *Tales of Folk and Faerie.* Jennet ran her fingers over the words, the letters cool to her touch.

"Another old book?" There was a smile in her dad's voice. "Jennet has a top-end tablet, you know. Nobody reads those old, musty things any more."

"This book is only available in print," Thomas said. "It's special. Go ahead, open it."

She lifted the cover, and caught her breath at the illustration on the opening page.

Moon-pale mushrooms encircled in a dusky glade, with

dark pines rising behind. Within the circle, small figures danced, winged and shining. The colors were rich and mysterious, and she could almost smell the resin of pine and cedar drifting from the page. The picture was titled *Midsummer Pixies*.

Fingers trembling, she turned the pages, titles of songs and stories flashing before her eyes: *The Elfin Knight, Childe Rolande, The Nixie*.

Most of the drawings were in black and white. Gnarled figures perched in tree branches, lovely women who called men to their deaths in deep water, winged sprites darting through a clearing. And the Black Knight. Jennet's stomach clenched as she stared at the picture of the knight. Her shoulder ached, and she hastily turned the page.

Next was a full-color illustration of a beautiful fey woman. Her face was delicate, her eyes deep and compelling. Her dress was woven of shadows and night. Pointed ears were just visible through her midnight-dark hair, gems tangled like stars in its silky blackness.

Her expression held a certain cruelty; something sharp in the tilt of her lips, her long-nailed fingers.

*The Faerie Queen.*

Shivering, Jennet closed the book.

"What do you think?" Thomas asked.

"I… it's amazing. Thank you."

"Keep it safe," he said. His smile was weary at the corners. "It's very valuable."

She hugged the book to her chest, her mind whirring. Pieces clicked into place like clockwork. Thomas: hired on to develop a top-secret game project for VirtuMax. Feyland: the game her dad was project manager for. And this book, full of ancient faerie lore that clearly was the inspiration for the world she had just been in.

Yet she couldn't say anything. She knew, with a bone-deep certainty, that Dad would forbid her to play Feyland again if she confessed she'd snuck on to the system. He would change his passwords, locking her out of that vividly magical world.

After dinner, she excused herself. Claiming she had too much homework, she went up to her room and pored over the book, absorbing every bit of information. Fynnoderee was a brownie from Manx lore. The Pixies were mischievous creatures, but not malicious. She found no mention of the Black Knight, though a dim memory of some ancient ballad hovered at the back of her mind.

Jennet read a short fable of a girl who entered an enchanted faerie ring on Midsummer's Eve, and found herself transported to the Realm of Faerie. She had feasted and danced—and when she returned to the real world the next morning, seventy human years had passed, and everyone she loved was dead.

It was brilliant, how Thomas had woven faerie lore into the game interface, and how VirtuMax brought it to virtual life. In a way, using the sim equipment was like stepping through a magical portal into another world.

Anticipation burned in her blood. Tomorrow, as soon as she got home from school, she'd return to Feyland and see what new adventures awaited.

IN THE MOON-DEEP clearing of the Dark Court, the queen sat silently on her throne. She turned a hollow glass sphere between her elegant hands; a vessel, waiting to be filled. Her Realm was withering, but the means to save it was nearly within her grasp.

The old ways had closed; the circles tumbled and broken, the wild places lost. But as long as she ruled the Dark Realm, she would fight for a return to the human world.

Midnight wind lifted her hair, the dark strands tarnished silver by starlight. Centuries of patience honed her to stillness as she bided. Soon. Soon.

A shiver ran through the court, and the queen smiled. That smile could cut to the bone, and the creatures nearest her throne cowered.

"Huntsman," she called. "I charge you—seek out your quarry in the mortal realm."

The antlered form of the Huntsman detached himself from the dark trees.

"I shall call the hounds," he said in a voice pulled from nightmare. "Tonight, the Wild Hunt rides."

"Do not let her escape."

"My queen." He bowed, his antlers sweeping a shadow across the moon.

Turning, he let out a piercing whistle. Feral red-eyed hounds flowed to him from the shadows, lithe and deadly. Behind them came the riders, white-haired elfin knights upon flame-footed horses. Without a word they leapt into the sky, blotting out the stars with their passage.

The eerie winding of the horn unfurled through the night. Small animals curled tighter in their dens. Any unfortunate, wakeful creature felt panic freeze their blood at the baying of the hounds and the thundering of hooves as the Hunt was loosed.

Jennet woke ten minutes before her alarm. Her skin was clammy from sweat, and the aftermath of weird, confused dreams echoed in her head. In fact, she didn't feel at all well. She stumbled out of bed and pulled on her robe, then hit the intercom button in her room.

"Marie?"

"Yes, Miss Jennet," the house manager said in her clipped accent. "I'll send your tea right up."

Jennet had been thinking of staying home from school, but maybe a cup of tea would perk her up, chase the last tatters of uneasy dreams from her head.

By the time George, their chauffeur, dropped her off at Prep, she felt better. The normalcy of the school day folded around her. The aggravations of her classes, the tight silence between herself and her former best friend, Taree—not pleasant, but at least familiar.

At lunch, Jennet sat alone at the end of a long table. Until last month, she and Taree had claimed this corner as their own. But now Taree was with a new boyfriend, one that Jennet couldn't stand. She'd been a little too honest about that with her former friend, and Taree had stopped talking to her.

Petro was rich, even by Prep standards, where the kids came from wealthy families. He was also mean, constantly picking on the 'shippers, the few scholarship students admitted to their elite school. Jennet wished she had the courage to say something, but getting on Petro's bad side meant nothing but trouble for everyone involved. If she had any hope of mending her friendship with Taree, she'd have to bite her tongue and wait for things to work out.

However, her sympathy didn't extend far enough to welcome the company of one of the 'shippers, when the tangle-haired girl set her lunch down next to Jennet. Didn't the girl know what a hairbrush was for? Jennet bolted the rest of her food and got up, leaving the girl to eat her meal alone.

Jennet went into the courtyard and found a bench in the shade. Closing her eyes, she conjured up memories of playing Feyland. She could hardly wait to get back in-game and shed the unhappiness creeping over her.

"Uh, hi." The unsteady voice broke into her musing.

Great. Brock Havers, the most annoying geeklet in school. For a second, Jennet contemplated faking sleep, but he'd just poke at her until she responded. With a sigh, she opened her eyes.

"Hey," she said.

Brock smiled, his eyes painfully full of unrequited love. "So, Jennet. I was just, uh. Anyway. There's that new movie?"

"I'm busy this week," she said. And next week. And next year.

"Oh, right." His expression clouded and he scuffed the gray concrete with his boot. Then he looked at her again, his eyes brightening. "Like, beta-testing for your dad or something I bet. Right? Isn't there a new top-secret game going into production?"

Jennet couldn't decide if Brock had a bigger crush on her, or on her connection to VirtuMax. She'd destroyed him in a school-organized sim tournament earlier that year, and ever since he'd followed her around as if he were a lost puppy. He didn't take hints, either.

"So, are you free this summer?" he asked. "Because soon as

school's done, I'm organizing a gaming club. If you joined it would be so prime. We'll have lots of fun."

"I bet."

"Like, my dad said he'd take us to SimCon to see Spark Jaxley!"

The celebrity gamer was a fixture in all of VirtuMax's ads, her signature magenta hair flying as she flawlessly met any challenge the sim systems threw at her. Jennet understood the appeal, but it wasn't worth having to spend all summer with Brock just to meet the gaming superstar.

"I have to work this summer," she lied. "My Dad's developing a new game, and I'm helping pre-beta it."

"Oh." Brock's eyes widened and he looked even more worshipful. "You're so lucky."

"Yeah."

If *luck* meant being practically an orphan in her own home.

Ah well, she'd learned to deal with the fact her mom had taken off years ago, and accept her workaholic dad with his messed-up priorities. At least she was surrounded by the best tech money could buy, attentive staff, and awesome games. And now she had Feyland.

The bell rang, a discreet ping signaling the end of lunch. Jennet stood and slung her satchel over one shoulder.

"See you," she said.

Before Brock could reply, she strode away. The force of his adoration always made her feel guilty, like she was a bad person for not finding him appealing in return. He wasn't a total loser. There was somebody out there for him—it just wasn't her.

Too bad the guy she was interested in didn't seem to know

she existed. Kenzer was a year ahead of her in school. He wasn't in any of her classes, but he lived in her neighborhood. She sometimes saw him at the g-board park or getting snacks at the corner store, but the most she'd ever done was muster up the courage to say hello. He'd nodded back, and that was it. Still, she couldn't help watching for him in the halls of Prep. The sight of his dark unruly hair, crooked smile, and blue eyes always made her heart beat faster.

No sign of Kenzer today, though. The wood-paneled walls absorbed the echoes of yelling students, but this close to the end of school, the excitement was palpable. One more week until summer break. And with Taree not talking to her, and no real boyfriends in sight, Jennet was more than glad to have the sweet distraction of Feyland waiting.

She could spend all summer exploring the game. Plenty of time when Dad was at work, and she knew the staff wouldn't say anything. Especially since they didn't have any way of knowing exactly *what* she was doing in the gaming room.

THE SCENT of roses and blood filled the clearing housing the Dark Queen's court. The queen waited upon her throne of knotted midnight, her sharp nails shredding the curling, dark vines beneath one hand. As though alive, the throne shivered in protest.

Behind the throne, a willowy creature with mossy hair played upon a flute, accompanied by the slow, solemn beats of a gnarled drummer, the pulse filling the spaces between the air. Waiting.

An eerie light filled the sky, and the queen lifted her head.

She slashed her hand across the darkness and the mournful music stopped, letting the sound of hounds and hooves penetrate the night. The Wild Hunt had returned.

The clearing filled, the sinuous bodies of the hounds flowing like black water, the red-eyed horses lathered and snorting. And riding majestic, the Huntsman.

"Where is my prize?" the queen asked, in a voice boding thunderstorms.

"My lady." The Huntsman dismounted and bowed, so low his antlered helm brushed the carpet of moss. "We cannot break through to the mortal world. The chink has been sealed."

"What?" The Dark Queen's voice cracked through the night, a whip felt across the breadth of her Realm. A killing frost swept the air, and the moss shriveled, flecked with diamonds of cold. The Huntsman did not straighten.

"We could not make our way into the places humans inhabit. The girl is lost to us."

"I will not allow it. Our salvation lies within reach—and I will *not* let it slip away." The queen rose, her pale face promising doom to any who met her eyes. "Watch for the mortal girl's presence. The moment a trace of her is felt, come to me."

"As you command."

The Huntsman, wise to the ways of his liege, backed away slowly, never once looking upon the queen's beautiful, terrible face.

The queen drew forth from the starry depths of her gown her long black thorn, honed to a killing point. Her fingers caressed it, moon-white against its darkness.

All protections against the Realm of Faerie eventually

failed—and this one had to have been hastily made, at best. The human world would open again to them, soon.

"MeadowRue," the queen said, beckoning to one of her handmaidens.

She would set a trap, while they waited. One that the human girl could not escape. The mortal would return and blunder into the queen's snares.

And when she did, the Realm would take what was necessary.

FOR THE NEXT WEEK, Jennet didn't get a chance to sneak back onto the FullD. Studying for finals squeezed out almost all her free time, thoughts of the game nibbling at her concentration. To distract herself, she watched some vids, took her g-board out in the waning light, and generally tried not to think too much about when she could get back into Feyland.

Still, she finished the year with good grades, despite her distraction. The day after school ended, she slept late and woke up smiling.

Their chef had made scones and left them with a bowl of fresh strawberries, on the dining room table. George, their chauffeur, messaged her tablet to let her know he was available if she wanted to go anywhere, and even Marie, the tight-faced house manager, unbent enough to offer her a cup of tea.

An hour later, Jennet was in the plush quiet of the computer room, belly full, door locked, and the whole day stretched gloriously before her. She flipped the FullD power on and geared up, then settled into the sim chair.

What awaited? Was the Black Knight still stationed outside

the ruined tower, sword poised to run her through? If so, she'd be ready.

Adrenaline spiking, she gave the command to enter game. The music sounded a fanfare, but this time there was no dizzying golden light, just a flare of white. Jennet's avatar materialized in the center of a clearing surrounded by birch trees, a faerie ring of tiny tan mushrooms around her feet. There was no sign of the dark woods, or the ruin—or the Black Knight.

She turned a slow circle to make sure, then let herself relax, tension flowing out of her shoulders. Sunlight dappled the green mosses beneath her feet, and the trees swayed in the slight wind.

A wind she couldn't feel.

Jennet frowned and dropped to her knees. Putting her face to the ground, she inhaled deeply. Nothing. No scent of herbs and flowers, not even the brown smell of soil. The programmers obviously hadn't worked the full range of sensory detail into this level of the game. It was a little disappointing.

Jennet stood again, then followed the path winding out of the clearing. The trees were richly detailed, but not as perfectly rendered as the ones in the first level of the game. Still, Feyland was a beautiful, enchanted world—far removed from her mundane life.

The path brought her to another clearing in the woods, larger than the first. The perfectly blue sky arched over a small meadow dotted with golden flowers. On the far side was a granite boulder, the grey stone sparkling with flecks of mica. Atop the stone sat a petite maiden in a yellowish gown, combing out her long dark hair. Her ears were sharply pointed.

A reassuring green glow surrounded the figure. Jennet guessed the aura surrounding the maiden signaled that she was friendly. Not that Jennet was taking any chances. Spells at the ready, she strode forward.

"Greetings," she said.

The maiden stopped combing her hair. "Greetings, brave adventurer," she said in a high, sweet voice. "Have you come to aid my people?"

"What aid do they require?" Jennet asked.

This dialogue was much more along the usual lines—a clear script to follow, unlike the weird interactions she'd had with Fynnod.

"Alas, my village has been suffering the attacks of bogles. Will you help defeat them?"

"I will."

A chime sounded in the air. Quickly, Jennet toggled open her game interface, to see that she had accepted a quest called "Bogle Battle."

Maybe the programmers hadn't done a spectacular job with the graphics in this level of the game, but the NPC inter-action and storyline was much stronger here. Probably the result of different teams working independently on the various parts of Feyland, then swapping around.

The maiden lifted a delicate hand and pointed to where the path continued past the boulder.

"My village lies yonder. Tell them Mustard Blossom sent you. Many thanks and a fine reward will be yours, if you prevail."

She picked up her comb again, and the green glow surrounding her faded. Her part was clearly done—though Jennet didn't think too highly of the programmer who made a character that sat around on rocks and did her personal grooming while her home was being attacked.

Then again, not everything in a game made sense, and at least this level was easier to follow. Jennet headed past the boulder and down the path.

The trees thinned, and beyond them was a small collection of whitewashed cottages. As she got closer to the mini-village, she saw a huddle of petite, sharp-eared figures beside the path. Three of them were weeping while one, a taller male, had his arms folded. He, too, bore the telltale green glow of a friendly NPC.

"Hi," Jennet said to him. "Mustard Blossom sent me to help."

He nodded. "We are in dire need. The bogles are rampaging in yonder field, and we fear our village will be next."

"I'm on it."

She turned off the path and headed through the first field, where golden stalks of grain waved softly in the breeze. When she came to the end of that field, she paused.

Ahead of her lay a ruined field—the grain trampled and blackened, as if from fire or blight. In the middle were four squat figures wearing rough leather armor and carrying wickedly sharp pikes. The bogles. A reddish glow outlined their figures, and they didn't seem to have spotted her yet.

Four against one. She didn't like the odds, but it didn't look as if any of the cowering villagers were going to help her. Her first real battle, and she was on her own. Jennet's pulse buzzed with adrenaline.

She'd start with her big opener; Wall of Flame. Sure, then she'd have four hot, irate bogles attacking, but she doubted she could pick them off singly. They were standing so close together that damaging one would alert the others.

The trick would be to keep moving, staying out of their weapon range while doing as much damage as possible. As a cloth-wearing Spellcaster, she was a "squishy" character, an easy pincushion for the bogles' sharp spears.

Jennet stepped back, finding the farthest range for her spellcasting. Charred wheat stubble crackled beneath her feet. Mentally crossing her fingers for luck, she lifted her staff and sent out her Wall of Flame. The air shimmered with heat and flame as her spell raced toward the bogles. Before it hit, she conjured a Fireball and flung it at the closest bogle.

The two spells reached the bogle simultaneously, and with a screech it fell to the ground. The remaining three turned, searching for their attacker. They spotted her and began yelling, their cries hoarse and guttural. The two nearest her brandished their pikes and sprinted forward, while their companion lagged behind. She really hoped that last one wasn't a magic-user.

Jennet raced away from her enemies at an angle, casting spells behind her. The lagging bogle raised his arms, red flames dancing at his fingertips. Not good. Hating to pause, Jennet whirled and took careful aim. Just as the bogle's spell formed, her Arcane Blast took him out—but she'd lost her lead on the other two bogles.

Forcing her hands to a steadiness she didn't feel, Jennet sent another Fireball at the closest one, then turned and ran.

The creatures were gaining—the rasp of their breathing scraped the air behind her. She put on a burst of speed to keep from getting a spear in the back, then pivoted and fired a blue bolt of arcane energy at her closest pursuer.

He halted, grunted, then slowly folded over. Before he hit the ground, his body disappeared. The other two bogle's bodies were gone, too.

Which left one angry bogle still at her heels. Jennet tilted her staff, ready to cast another Fireball, but she'd misjudged. The last bogle was too close, the wicked barbs of his weapon thrusting right for her head.

Heart pounding, she ducked, reflexively raising her staff. Metal met wood with a jar she felt down to her shoulders. The bogle grunted, then pulled his pike back, ready for another jab.

Jennet danced back and sent the glowing orb of a Fireball toward her opponent. The bogle leaped out of the way, then rushed her, his sharp teeth glinting in a cruel smile.

Grabbing the end of her staff with both hands, Jennet swung it like a baseball bat, putting all her strength behind the blow. The bogle's eyes went wide at her unexpected move, and he couldn't get his pike up in time to block her attack.

Her staff connected with his leather armor, then kept going, meeting no resistance as her final foe disappeared. The force of her swing pulled her around in a half-circle, and she staggered, finally catching her balance.

The field was empty of bogles.

She'd done it—though not as gracefully as she might have liked. Triumphant music drifted through the air as the inhabitants of the tiny village hurried toward her. Their delicate faces were smiling, and the leader carried a heavy sack.

"Bold adventurer," he said, bowing to her. "You saved our village. We can never repay you—but please take these gold coins as a token of our gratitude."

"You're welcome," she said, taking the sack.

The moment it was in her hands, it disappeared with a clinking sound. Curious, she toggled open her game interface to see that she now had one hundred gold coins in her inventory. Nice. No doubt they would come in handy.

"Will you take word of your victory to the forest camp?" the leader asked, gesturing to a small road leading away from the village. "Our kin there will be glad to hear of it."

"Sure," Jennet said. The NPC continued to look at her, so she changed her wording. "I will."

This time, the man nodded to her, and she heard the chime that signaled she'd accepted a new quest.

"Be careful on your travels," the leader said. "Many dangerous creatures lurk within the forest and prey upon the unwary. Farewell!"

He waved, and the villagers bowed to her—her cue to go.

It was time for her to stop playing, anyway, and the road seemed a good place for her to exit Feyland. Jennet strode away from the small village. When she reached the pale, dusty road, she lifted her fingers in the command to log out.

THE WEEKS FLEW PAST, and Jennet felt as though she was living two lives—the depressingly mundane one of Jennet Carter, and the rich, lively adventures of Fair Jennet in Feyland. She'd faced off against ogres, fought basilisks, spoken with ethereally beautiful faerie maidens, and completed some of the strangest quests. Things like sorting out a big pile of lentils and rice, or falling down a well and talking to animals.

There was one creature who kept showing up, a Non-Player-Character with ratty hair and a tattered dress who tried to get Jennet to do pointless quests. The creature reminded Jennet too uncomfortably of the 'shipper girl at school, so she tried to avoid the NPC whenever possible. Easy enough to do—the world of Feyland was full of levels and layers. Completing the Deep Forest had taken her most of a week, and that was with hours a day in-game.

When Jennet wasn't playing Feyland, she was thinking about it. She spent the evenings poring over *Tales of Folk and Faerie*, so much that Dad even noticed.

Thomas came over for dinner a few times, and Jennet couldn't help asking him questions about the book; trying to find out what she could about Feyland without being obvious. He gave her searching looks, but answered. Sometimes the answer made no sense, but she didn't want to push it. Thomas was suspicious enough as it was.

Weekends were the worst. Barred from her secret FullD playing, she wasted time on Screenie games and counted the hours until Dad left for work again. Once, she messaged Taree, but her ex-friend didn't bother responding. So much for that.

The only other thing for her to do was take her g-board out. Their neighborhood had a local park with half-pipes and ramps. She wasn't the best boarder, but she knew some tricks —which put her in the uncomfortable, solitary ground between the newbies and the prime riders.

When she arrived at the park, she made a quick scan for Kenzer. Her heart gave a crazy bump when she saw him at the far side, doing half-flips with ease. The afternoon light gleamed off his helmet, and she squinted, trying to see his face.

This time she'd talk to him.

But by the time she worked up her nerve to go over, he'd merged with a group of his friends and they were already heading out, talking and laughing as they left the concrete half-pipes and ramps behind. Jennet clutched her g-board, the edges digging into her hands, and watched as Kenzer and the others piled into a new-model grav-car. The car lifted smoothly and pulled away.

So much for that. At least the park was quieter now, with fewer kids to notice as she tried out some new moves. An hour later, the sun was low enough to make her squint every time she turned around. Still, it hadn't been a total waste. She'd figured out the board-flip move, even if she had a few bruises to show for it.

When she got home, she stowed her board and headed to the kitchen for a glass of water. After that, she needed a shower to wash the faint stickiness of sweat off her skin and hair.

"Jennet?" her dad called as she passed the open study door, "could you come in here, please?"

Apprehension zinged through her, drying her throat. Had he found out she'd been sneaking onto the FullD?

"Sure." She tried to keep her voice nonchalant.

She stepped into the room and perched on one of the blue upholstered chairs facing the desk. Lacing her hands together, she gave her dad a smile meant to look innocent.

"I have some news." He paused and rubbed the bridge of his nose.

Something jagged and bright flashed through her. Had he actually heard from her mother, after all these years? She leaned forward. Sunlight sliced through the slatted blinds at the window, falling like promises across the disheveled papers on his desk.

"VirtuMax wants to relocate all the senior employees," he said, and Jennet sat back, swallowing disappointment. Not her mother. Never her mother.

"Relocate? To where?"

Maybe it would be a big city, or somewhere with beaches. Middland was all right, as far as medium-sized cities went, but there were more exciting places to live in the world.

"Crestview," he said.

Jennet felt her brows pull together. "Crestview? Where's that? I've never even heard of it."

"Not many people have." He steepled his fingers and gave her a weary smile. "It's in the middle of the country, a smallish city compared to here. But the backbone of the 'net runs right through, making it ideal for VirtuMax."

Probably the podunk little town had offered bribes and incentives, too. After all, VirtuMax was the biggest gaming company in the world.

"I don't really want to move." Not that she had a lot going on here, but Prep was a great school, and she loved singing in the concert youth choir. Eventually she and Taree would start speaking again. And how would Kenzer ever notice her if she left?

"I don't want to be separated from you, Jennet, but I don't want to uproot you, either. Prep has a boarding option."

"Wait, you'd just leave me here? Alone?" The thought rose up to choke her. She'd already had one parent abandon her.

"Honey. I only want what's best for you. I'd miss you a lot, but Crestview doesn't have much to recommend it. VirtuMax is building an intentional neighborhood for the staff—but right now very few of the amenities are in place. Until the VirtuMax school is built, you'd have to attend the local high school. There's no choir, none of the kind of cultural activities you're used to."

Great. Accept abandonment, or go with Dad to the backside of nowhere. Neither choice appealed.

"I'll think about it."

He nodded. "It's still a few months out. We'll figure it out."

She didn't want to figure it out. She wanted to crawl back inside the game, where winning was practically guaranteed, and where troubles didn't cling to her like viscous shadows, darkening everything.

"All right," she said. Though it wasn't.

ADDING TO JENNET'S FRUSTRATION, her dad caught a summer cold that kept him home for a solid week. Though her head itched and her fingers burned with the desire to play Feyland, she couldn't risk logging into the FullD system. Even when Dad was napping.

Once he felt a little better, Thomas came to visit. The three of them sat in the living room, drinking cups of minty tea. Jennet scuffed at the patterned oriental rug with the toe of her shoe, wishing she could ask him about Feyland.

"Dr. Lassiter was inquiring when you'll be back to work," Thomas said to her dad. "She doesn't want the project to fall behind."

"I've messaged her every day," Dad said. "Asking *you* isn't going to make me miraculously better." He paused to cough, then took a sip of tea. "I should be back next Monday. And we're not going to fall behind. We don't have the time."

Thomas nodded, and a look passed between the two men that Jennet couldn't decipher. She wrapped her hands around her mug and studied Thomas. He didn't look that great, himself; pale and strained, and thinner than the last time he'd been over.

"Are you okay?" she asked.

Surprise flashed over his face before he covered it with a tight smile. "I'm fine."

"Maybe coming down with my cold," Dad said at the same time.

"Maybe so," Thomas said, after a too-long second. He gulped his tea and rose. "I'll see you at work. Lunch as usual on Monday?"

"Of course." Her dad half-rose as Thomas stood to leave.

"No, don't get up." Thomas waved him back onto the couch. "You rest. And Jennet," he turned to her, "stay out of trouble."

"Always do." Since there was pretty much zero trouble she could get into in their upscale neighborhood, with the house staff watching, and her game access denied. She took a sip of her cooling tea. "I'll see you out."

At the door, Thomas took her by the shoulder. "I'm serious. If you're—"

"One more thing," her dad called, moving slowly out of the living room. "If you need something to mollify Dr. Lassiter, tell her the techs are ready to code the next level."

Thomas nodded. He squeezed Jennet's shoulder and let his hand drop heavily to his side.

"You two take care." He stepped outside, into the too-warm brightness of the summer afternoon.

For a moment he was outlined in light, a brilliant flare that made Jennet blink. Then it was just Thomas, thin and weary, walking out to his car. She and Dad stood together, watching until Thomas pulled away. The smell of fresh-cut lawn swirled into the house, and Jennet's dad sighed.

"What's wrong?" she asked.

"Just work stuff. I'm going to lie down for a bit."

Pressing her lips together in worry, Jennet didn't push him. Couldn't push. Her words were leashed inside her, demands and arguments she'd swallowed for a dozen years.

Even though she and Dad never talked about it, she knew why her mother had left when she was four. She still dimly recalled her yelling tantrum, the last straw that had driven her mother away.

Sure, Dad had taken her to expensive therapy, but the shame still bound her, the secret knowledge that she had been so terrible her own mother had fled. So she didn't argue, didn't talk back, just went up to her bedroom and watched stupid vids until she was too tired to think.

By Monday, her dad felt well enough to go back to work. Jennet waved goodbye a little too enthusiastically, then ran up to the computer room. A few minutes later she was in-game. This time, golden light enveloped her, sending dizzy spirals through her stomach.

It reminded her of the first time she'd played.

She'd mastered six levels since then—each one with interesting challenges. There had been puzzles to unlock, and ferocious fights, and plenty of the usual hack-and-grind questing she was used to from other games. Sometimes Feyland threw odd twists at her, but after that first, creepy start, things had normalized.

No question that the game had patchy coding, which was to be expected of a pre-beta prototype. It was obvious the techs had concentrated their efforts at the beginning. After those first couple quests in-game, the experience had flattened out; the sensations not as vivid or immersive. Though it was still an amazing game.

Jennet's avatar materialized, as usual, in a faerie ring—but this time she was in the center of a circle of moon-pale mushrooms. Tall oaks encircled the clearing, and the sky was an indigo curtain, dusted silver with stars. A sweet night wind ruffled her hair, pulled at the skirt of her gown—and she *felt* it. There was an extra-reality to the sensations enfolding her. The taste of dew tingled on her tongue, the soft mosses gave like plush velvet beneath her feet.

Clearly the programmers had concentrated on the endgame, too—which meant she was getting close to the final boss.

"She comes!" The wood-colored spriggan bowed before the queen, spindly limbs trembling to be this close to her darkness.

"At last." The queen's smile was a blade, her eyes black chasms.

The spriggan shook like bare branches in the winter wind. He was the least of his clan, and fully expected to be seized in those pale, deadly hands, broken into kindling, and thrown on the violet bonfire flickering behind him, his screams mixing with the flames as his essence was consumed.

But the queen dismissed him with a gesture, beckoning instead to one of her gossamer-clad handmaidens.

"Greenbriar," she said.

The faerie maiden bowed her head, hair like moonlight dipping over her face, and moved with willowy grace to stand before the queen. Rising, the Dark Queen took Greenbriar's hand and pulled her close. The blackthorn dagger pulsed in the queen's pale grasp, an absence of light, of hope.

With one swift move, the queen plunged the thorn into her handmaiden's chest, stabbing her to the heart. Greenbriar let out a keening cry that rose up until the stars themselves shuddered. Shaped by the queen's need, powered with fresh-spilled faerie blood, the Realm opened an inexorable path beneath the mortal girl's feet.

Hollow and lifeless, Greenbriar's body fell to the mute grasses, her pale hair spread out around her like snow. Goblins hastened to bear her away. The musicians struck up a dirge, and the queen tucked her deadly thorn back into her gown.

"Now," she said in a voice hard as diamond, "we await our guest."

JENNET DREW in a breath of the night-deep air, chill with the faint memory of shuttered flowers. Above, the sky was pricked with stars, and the thin sliver of a crescent moon tangled in the dark branches of the oaks. She'd never been here before, and her heart sped with the lure of the new. The path wound between tall, night-shadowed trees, their branches gilded with silver light.

Her mage staff shed its usual blue glow, tingeing the shadows azure. Some night creature called, then went still. The wind shifted and for a moment she thought she heard music, flute and drum, borne on the air.

No question this was one of the most immersive levels of Feyland. She hadn't felt the sensory input this keenly since her first adventures in-game. A smile sparked through her, moving up from her feet until it found her face, and stayed.

The path led her smoothly on—no briars or brambles to snare her feet, no sudden enemies leaping from the shadows. Ahead, she glimpsed flickers of violet flame. Music threaded between the trees, the flute and drum now joined by a fiddle in a tune that made her want to dance.

This was it. Something important lay ahead. The final challenge of Feyland.

Her smile faded. If it was, what happened when she defeated the last boss and finished the game?

Of course she'd roll a new character and experience it all over again, but nothing ever compared to that first time through.

Motes of light glimmered ahead, beckoning. Jennet set aside her bittersweet thoughts and went forward. Whatever happened, she was here now. She was ready.

The trees opened to form a clearing. In the center a garish purple bonfire burned, disjointed figures capering about it. Beneath the canopy of trees on one side, long tables were set, spread with delicacies. Candles in huge silver candelabra illuminated gem-crusted goblets and sharp-edged knives. Creatures from dream and nightmare feasted there, many of whom she recognized from the pages of Thomas's book: sprites and banshees, goblins and phoukas.

Silken-winged creatures with sharp teeth swooped and darted above the crowd, and laughter chimed like bells. A trio of musicians played just beyond the tables, the music frothing and spinning beneath the sky. The moon had won free of the trees and now hung, a radiant scythe harvesting the dark.

Jennet took a step into the clearing, away from the shelter of the trees. Silence crashed down, like a door suddenly slamming. The fey folk turned toward her, their eyes avid.

Fear clogged Jennet's throat. There was no way she could fight them all. But they made no move to unsheathe weapons or attack. From the nearby shadows, a spindly figure approached. Jennet lifted her staff, spells at her fingertips.

"Fair Jennet," the creature creaked in a voice like long-dry wood. "Welcome to the Dark Court. Our queen awaits you."

"Is it… safe?" The question caught in her throat.

The figure laughed. "The court is never safe. But the Dark Queen has given you leave to pass."

His words broke the spell of silence binding the company. The musicians struck up again, and the fey folk turned back to their feasting, though Jennet could still see their feral glances and sly smiles turned her way.

"Come." The creature gestured with oddly-jointed limbs, then led her around the bonfire.

At the far end of the clearing sat a throne of night-black vines And upon that throne…

*The Faerie Queen.*

Her black hair framed a pale face as hard and exquisite as ice. Her gown, made of tattered midnight, stirred in an unfelt breeze. Her eyes were deep pools of starlight and shadow, fathomless, promising everything—and nothing.

Jennet met the queen's gaze. Her breath caught in her throat, burned her lungs, as though she had opened the freezer and accidentally taken a deep breath of frigid air.

Gasping, she tore her eyes away. Pain crimped her side. The queen was dangerous. Beyond dangerous. And this was Feyland's final combat; Jennet felt it in her bones.

"Fair Jennet," the queen said, the barest wisp of a smile on her beautiful, pitiless face. "You think to best me in battle?"

"I plan on it." Jennet shook off the doubts, cold as snow, that settled on her shoulders.

"Very well," the queen said. "I accept your challenge."

Jennet couldn't see any weapons on her opponent, and that dress was no substitute for armor. This was going to be a magical duel, then; spell-caster against spell-caster. She flexed her fingers around the smooth wood of her staff. Anticipation spiked through her. She could do this.

The fey folk left their feasting tables and encircled her and the queen in a loose ring. From the corner of her eye, Jennet saw red-eyed hounds and the shadow of antlers rising against the dark trees. She swallowed a shiver and focused back on the Dark Queen.

A figure stepped forward from the obsidian shadows behind the throne—a knight clad all in black, tall and forbidding. Jennet couldn't contain the prickle of fear tightening her skin.

The Black Knight. If she had to fight him, she was in severe trouble.

He held his gauntleted fist high and grated out a single word. "Begin."

It echoed eerily through the glade, and the fey folk let out a rough cheer. There was no one to cheer for Jennet.

Without hesitation, she tipped her staff and shot a bolt of mage-light at the queen. A sphere of shadow appeared, blocking Jennet's attack and swallowing the fire into its dark depths. More spheres materialized and began floating toward her, called by the Dark Queen. Jennet ducked and wove, avoiding their deadly touch.

Lightning crackled from her staff, illuminating the clearing with shocking white light, but the queen evaded her bolts. Still, Jennet kept pressing the attack. The dark spheres were multiplying now, bobbing in the air on all sides. A low, menacing hum surrounded her as she tried to find a clear shot.

She couldn't afford any mistakes—but the fight was pushing her to her limits. Worry nibbled at the edges of her concentration. She just had to watch for an opening... there. She took aim and sent another bolt crackling through the air.

White fire sizzled and Jennet heard the queen gasp. Yes! She could do it. She could beat this game. The first player ever to claim victory over Feyland.

A dark sphere brushed against her shoulder. Frost stabbed into her skin, sent numbness down her arm until she could barely hold onto her staff. She stumbled back, trying to regain the rhythm of the battle. Keep breathing. Keep fighting. But where was the queen? The place where her opponent had stood was now filled with twisting shadows.

Everything rippled, as though the clearing was made of cloth billowing in a sudden gust. Jennet heard high, chiming laughter as she fell backward...

And landed in an ornate chair set before a feasting table.

*What?* She jumped up, heart racing, and knocked the edge of the table. A goblet sitting in front of her shook, sending a drop of deep red liquid to stain the white tablecloth.

"Sit down, Fair Jennet," the queen said from her place across the table. "This is the next stage of our battle."

Pale candles in thorny candelabra illuminated the feast. Their silver flames reflected in the queen's fathomless eyes.

"You changed the rules! You can't do that." Jennet's legs felt shaky as she edged back into her chair. She was so not prepared for this.

The queen laughed. It was the sound of ice shattering on a black lake. "Of course I can. This is my court. My realm. You are but a visitor. Please—drink." She waved one delicate hand at the goblet.

"No, thanks."

Jennet's mouth said the words, but her hand reached out anyway and lifted the heavy silver goblet. A sweet, thick smell drifted from the cup. Roses and burnt sugar. The edge of metal touched her lips.

No. She was not going to do this. The queen might try to control their battle, but she could still fight back. Fingers trembling from effort, Jennet forced the goblet away. The air around her was sticky and nearly solid, like dough. She pushed against it, her breath coming in gasps, until at last the cup touched the table.

"Very well." The queen's voice was edged with frost. "If you disdain my hospitality, then you must answer a riddle."

That seemed safer than drinking whatever was in the goblet. And the game wasn't giving her a lot of other options. "A riddle? All right."

The candles flared and the queen's eyes glowed. "Listen

then, and listen well, the answer to this riddle tell, or forfeit of thyself will be, and never more wilt thou be free."

Jennet shivered. The queen's voice was ominous, her words intoned with deep meaning. Whatever happened, it was clear that failing to answer the riddle carried a price. Jennet curled her fingers tightly into her palms and tried not to show the fear flickering through her.

"Ask me your riddle," she said.

"As soon as it begins, it is ending. Without form, still it moves. When it is gone, it yet remains." The queen smiled, sharp as a blade. "You have three guesses."

"Ah…" Jennet's mouth was dry. Her mind beat against the riddle like a bird trapped behind glass. Without taste or form. Something powerful, but insubstantial. "Is it the wind?"

A low sighing went through the branches of the dark trees. The candle nearest her snuffed out, as though some invisible hand had abruptly doused the flame.

The queen shook her head. "One chance gone."

A circle of watchers had formed around the table. Lithe women with gossamer wings gathered beside the queen. Gnarled brown creatures with fingers that were too long for their hands swayed next to them. Red-capped goblins and capering sprites—they all watched her with avid, gleaming eyes.

Freaky. This whole battle had turned beyond strange. Jennet pulled in a deep breath, though her chest felt tight, and gave another answer. "Music?"

The second she said the word, she knew it was wrong. She shivered as a second candle flame went out. The watchers surrounding her tittered, and the low breeze rustled the branches.

"Two chances gone." The queen's words held a victorious edge. "A pity you have no allies in this."

She beckoned, and a faerie stepped up to her side—a beautiful maiden in a dress spun of cobwebs and dusk. Gossamer wings rose from her shoulders, changing hues in the wan light from blue to silver to palest violet.

"My handmaiden, MeadowRue," the queen said. "You have met before."

"I don't think so," Jennet said.

The Dark Queen smiled, an expression so sharp it could draw blood. "Ah yes. She wore a different form then."

The queen's pale fingers moved in a complex gesture, and the faerie maiden shrank and darkened, until a lumpish creature stood there, clad in a ragged dress with unkempt hair. Jennet sucked in a breath. It was the annoying creature who had kept wanting her to do dead-end quests! The one that had reminded her too much of the unfortunate scholarship girl at Prep. Damn it. Obviously she'd made a bad call there.

"Fair Jennet," the handmaiden said, her voice as thin and raspy as Jennet recalled. "Thrice I begged you for aid, and thrice you refused me. Had you but bent your grasping human ways, I would now be permitted to aid you. But your impatience and selfishness blinded you. Now, at your time of need, you must stand alone."

"But…"

Jennet caught her lower lip between her teeth. She wanted to argue, to beg for another chance, but there were no excuses. Not for the way she'd behaved in-game, and not for the way she'd treated the 'shipper girl. *Should-haves* writhed in the pit of her belly. Even in a game, she could have strived to be a better person. And definitely in real life.

With a wave of her hand, the queen restored MeadowRue to her true form. The handmaiden gave Jennet a glance full of pity, then turned away.

"The riddle remains," the queen said. "Answer it."

Jennet squeezed her eyes closed, blocking out the shadowy glade, the fantastical figures, the wicked curve of the Dark Queen's smile. Her heart thumped loudly in her chest, and she tasted the metal edge of fear on her tongue. Think. She had to figure this out.

"Your time has run, Fair Jennet. Speak your final answer."

She opened her eyes, to see that the Dark Queen had risen to her feet. A single candle burned between them.

"I..."

Panic banged through her, like a hundred doors slamming shut. The watching creatures grew still and silent. Even the wind quieted, waiting. She had to answer.

"Is it ... a dream?" The words floated from her mouth and hovered there, just beyond her lips.

In the silence that followed, Jennet felt shadows gathering closer. Dread crawled through her, carrying the awful sensation of failure.

The last candle died. A high, wailing music started up, the keening cry of pipes swirling through the air. Slowly, the queen shook her head. Diamonds sparkled like frost in her dark hair.

"No," she said. "You have lost. Now, mortal girl, I take my due."

The queen held up a hollow crystal sphere in one hand. With the other, she scribed strange gestures in the air. Her fingers left glowing streaks of silver against the darkness. Then she pointed straight at Jennet.

"Ahh!" A sharp pain speared through Jennet, as though the queen had stabbed her in the chest. She doubled over, gasping, while agony iced her blood. Oh god. It hurt.

"Behold, Fair Jennet," the queen said. "The answer is Life. Your essence is captured here. It will serve us well."

Jennet looked up, tears clouding her vision. The queen held the sphere aloft. It wasn't empty any more. Inside was a bright swirl of color, like rainbow flames. They pulsed and danced, trapped inside their crystal prison. Wavering, calling to her.

"How," Jennet forced the words out through lips tight with pain, "how do I get that back?"

Every game had a second chance, a third. You kept fighting the last battle until you finally won. Failure wasn't permanent. Not like in real life.

The queen laughed, and the sound carried a bitter chill. "You cannot. Without a champion, you are lost. Now go. Go! I send thee, defeated, from the Dark Realm."

Pain wrenched through Jennet and she screamed. Golden light blinded her senses and she swirled through a sickening vertigo. Blackness waited, merciful and dark, on the other side. She opened her arms to it, and fell.

JENNET WOKE, aching, in the sim chair. Her hands were stiff inside the gaming gloves, and when she sat forward, fire exploded in her shoulder. She could barely lift her arm, but it was impossible to take off the helmet one-handed. Trying not to whimper, she gritted her teeth against the agony and pulled off her gear.

She had lost.

Feyland was more than just a sim game. The clues had been there all along, but she hadn't paid enough attention until now. Now, when it was too late. And she'd done worse than lose the game.

There was a frigid hollow in the center of her chest. The Dark Queen had taken something from her—something she feared she couldn't live without. Bright flames trapped inside a magical sphere. Her *mortal essence*, the queen had said.

She had to get it back.

Jennet stumbled to her bedroom. She swayed at the edge of her bed, trying to pull the covers back. No use. She toppled forward onto the blue coverlet, and let the blackness of sleep take her down.

*C*ALL AN AMBULANCE! *Now!*

*...unusual symptoms, Mr. Carter. No signs of external trauma...*

*--still unconscious?*

*...as soon as she wakes up we'll notify you. Now get some rest...*

*(sobbing)*

"D*AD*?" Her voice was creaky, the word sticking in her mouth like it was coated with tar.

Jennet thought she'd heard him, his voice taut with panic. And later—crying? What was going on?

She couldn't open her eyes. And then she could, the lashes parting gummily. Unfamiliar white walls surrounded her, and the antiseptic smell hit her nose the same time her brain registered *hospital*.

What was she doing lying in a hospital bed?

An IV fed into her left arm, and she was dressed in a dun-colored gown. The gridded lights overhead made her want to close her eyes again, but she had to figure out what was going on.

"Dad?" she called again, fear lending her voice a wavery strength.

The door opened and a blue-smocked nurse bustled in, her hair tied neatly back.

"Awake at last," she said. "And how are you feeling?"

"I really don't know." Jennet took a deep breath. Nothing hurt, but her throat was blazingly parched. "Could I get some water?"

The nurse nodded. "I'll be right back. But if you need anything else, press the call button."

"I need my dad."

"Contacting him is the first thing on my list." The nurse gave her an encouraging smile and left, closing the door softly.

Jennet stared around the room. There was a big vase of hydrangeas—blue and purple and green—the only real spot of color in the place. Thick white curtains were drawn over the window, the light a bright smear behind.

The door flew open, and her dad rushed in. His hair was rumpled and he looked exhausted, but as soon as he saw her, a smile transformed his face.

"Jen! Oh, honey."

He caught her up in a hug, careful of the tubes stuck in her arm, and Jennet clung to him. He smelled like sunshine and safety.

"I'm here, Dad."

"I know." His voice was thick with emotion. "The docs say they want another day of observation, and then they'll let you come home. I can't believe I didn't realize you had walking pneumonia—I'm so sorry."

"I did?" She didn't remember being sick.

What she did remember was the Dark Queen taking her mortal essence—but that must have been a dream. Right? She had been feverishly ill, after all. The strange, hollow feeling in her chest was just an after-effect of her illness; nothing more.

"We're through it now," her dad said. Tears lurked in his eyes. "Let me get some light in here."

He went to the window and pulled back the curtain. Afternoon sun poured into the room, as though it had just been waiting for an invitation. The branches of a tree were visible from the bed, dark green leaves moving gently in the breeze below the cloud-spotted sky.

Returning to the bedside, her dad sat and took her hand.

"I have some bad news," he said, his voice strained. "It's… I don't know how to tell you this, but—Thomas is dead."

"What?" She clutched his hand, her mind buzzing in circles. "How could he be? What happened?"

Dad shook his head. "He died at home, the doctors think from a stroke. It was fast, and probably painless."

Tears choked her throat. "But I didn't get to say goodbye."

"None of us did." Her dad blinked, hard, but a drop of moisture still rolled down one cheek. "I'm so sorry to have to break this to you while you're still in the hospital, but I thought you'd want to know right away."

Jennet pressed her lips together and nodded. She couldn't quite believe that Thomas was gone.

"The funeral is the day after tomorrow. You'll be home by then." Her dad leaned forward again and wrapped her in a tight hug. "I love you," he said against her hair.

"I love you too, Dad." She hugged him awkwardly back, mindful of the IV.

She felt cold and empty inside, but at least she was alive, and with her dad. Thomas's death was horrible—but she and Dad had gone through worse and come out the other side.

Not perfectly, no, but who ever made it through life without a few scars?

THE DARK QUEEN paced the length of her court, her dress a shimmer of smoke and shadows, her midnight hair stirred by the ever-present night breeze. In one hand she held a crystal sphere where a small flame flickered. It was the barest ember of fire—but it was enough.

She had made a bargain, and she would remain true to it. The fey folk were ever bound by their word. But bargains were tricky things, and she had centuries of experience. The poor mortal who had thought to negotiate with her had gotten what he wanted, but at a price few would pay, and for a far shorter time than he believed.

The queen smiled, as bright and sharp as the stars over-head. In a swirl of night, she mounted her throne and settled into its tangled black depths. To one side stood a knot of musicians: a long-fingered creature with a wooden flute, a squat goblin holding a skin drum, and a sad-eyed man with a battered guitar slung across his back.

"Music," she said, gesturing to the players. "I would hear a song from my new Bard—something pleasant to pass the time. A tale of treachery and deceit, perchance."

The denizens of her court laughed, their cackles and gibbers echoing off the trunks of the tall oak trees. Pale moths fluttered away from the sound, wings beating like panicked hearts.

"As my lady commands."

The man set his fingers on the strings of his guitar, bowed his head, and began to play.

# HOW TO BABYSIT A CHANGELING

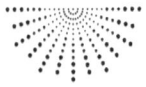

## A FEYLAND TALE

THE CAFETERIA at Crestview High was filled with the din of conversation, the clank of silverware on plasmetal trays, and somebody's tunes cranked up too loud, screeching tinnily out of their earbuds. Despite the noise, despite the smell of floor cleaner mixed with cooked cabbage, despite the fact that high school was all kinds of tedious, Marny Fanalua never let things get to her. It wasn't worth getting tangled up in small annoyances—and almost everything was small, when you took a breath and looked at it.

She sat across from her friends, slightly scruffy Tam Linn and rich-girl Jennet Carter. They'd all found out recently that life was a lot more interesting than they'd ever imagined.

A little *too* interesting at times, maybe. It wasn't every day a person discovered that their favorite sim video game was actually a portal into a treacherous magical world.

Marny leaned forward and rested her broad arms on the table, studying Tam's face. She'd known him a long time, and she could tell by the tightness around his eyes—what she could see of them behind the screen of his overlong brown hair—that something was severely wrong.

Wrong beyond the usual tweaked state of Tam's life, which was bad enough. Nobody could call scraping by in the Exe fun.

Maybe his mom had taken off again. In Marny's opinion the woman barely qualified for the title, other than the fact that she'd given birth to Tam and his little brother. So, either his mom had gone off her meds and left Tam and the Bug in the lurch again, or something freaky was going on.

And if it was something freaky, that meant magic. Fey magic.

"Okay, spill it," she said.

Jennet sent her a grateful half-smile, but Marny stayed focused on Tam. He clenched one hand, then smoothed it out flat over the scraped tabletop. Before speaking, he shot a quick glance at the neighboring tables, but nobody was paying attention to them. Why should they? She and Tam were misfits—always had been. And Jennet had become a lost cause to the status-conscious Viewer kids since becoming Tam's sort-of girlfriend.

"They've taken my little brother," Tam said, his voice tight.

Oh, crap. Marny narrowed her eyes. Tam's brother, the Bug, was a sweet kid, if a bit random.

"*They*, as in the Dark Court faeries?" she asked. Tam nodded, and coldness settled in the pit of her stomach. "How do you know?"

"I know because they left a changeling creature in his place." Tam swiped his hair out of his eyes. "My brother is being held hostage in the Realm of Faerie by the Dark Queen, in payback for Jennet and me meddling between the realms."

"Yeah well, your *meddling* is kind of crucial." Marny folded her arms. "It's keeping the fey from stealing human energy and opening a gateway to the mortal world. Stopping blood sacrifice. Little things like that."

"We never thought they could do something like this, though," Jennet said. "Tam's brother is in serious danger."

She would know, too, having encountered the queen a few times too many. The back of Marny's neck prickled. Personally, she was glad to have never encountered that particular being. One of the advantages of staying out of sim games. Especially Feyland, which had managed to use the game interface to open a gateway from the Realm of Faerie to the mortal world, with serious consequences.

"Also, my mom's gone again," Tam said, his gaze dropping to the dingy floor, as if it were his fault the woman had problems.

Double serving of trouble for Tam, then. Marny shook her head.

"How do we get your little brother out of Feyland?" she asked.

"We're working on that from the inside," Jennet said, laying one pale, slim hand on Tam's shoulder. "We'll get him back."

"Meanwhile there's a creature living in my house." Tam shoved his tray away, food uneaten. "I can't leave it there alone all the time."

Marny took a deep breath, instantly regretting it as the smell of overcooked spaghetti filled her nose.

"So, just to be clear—the Bug's been stolen away by the faeries, and they left a substitute in his place?" she asked. "One that's now living with you?"

Tam nodded miserably.

"I want to meet him. It. Whatever," Marny said, before she even knew the words were going to come out of her mouth. Yet, it made perfect sense for her to get involved.

"What?" Tam jerked his head up, denial flashing through his green eyes.

"Look." She spread her hands wide. "You two have to deal with things in-game. The last thing you need to worry about is some freaky faerie dude pretending to be the Bug. Even though I don't sim, I can help with this."

Jennet nodded and looked at Tam. "She's right. We can't take care of the changeling, and beta testing Feyland, and everything else that's going on—not by ourselves."

"At least your mom's not around," Marny said. "It's crappy that she's gone, but the timing is decent. Considering. This way, if she comes home and you guys are, um, unavailable, I can run interference."

Tam and Jennet needed to get back in-game to try and rescue the Bug. And Marny *had* encountered the magic and creatures of Feyland before. She was up for this.

Looking after the changeling thing couldn't be much worse than the few times she'd babysat Tam's actual little brother, right? That kid was a ball of crazy energy.

The hubbub in the cafeteria was dying down, the tables emptying out.

"Okay." Tam swiped a hand through his hair. He looked like he'd barely gotten any sleep. "Marny, if you're free you can come over after school today and meet the changeling. Provided it's still there."

"It will be," Jennet said. "I think changelings have to stay close to home. Their pretend home, I mean. I'll read up in my folklore book and let you know what else I find out."

"Good." Marny nodded, her black hair tickling her cheek. "This should be interesting."

Tam and Jennet could have their adventures inside Feyland.

Gaming was fine, and she was good at it, as long as she wasn't simming. But Marny had always felt that real life contained more than enough weirdness for a person to deal with. And she never had figured herself for hero material, anyway. Sure, she was competent and smart and strong, but there were better-qualified people when it came to saving the world.

IT WASN'T Marny's idea of a fun time, going on foot through the Exe—basically the ghetto of Crestview—but there was no other way to get to Tam's house. They'd met up after school and she followed him down stinking alleys, stepping over puddles slimed with oil and decay. Past graffiti-layered buildings with broken windows staring like blind eyes, and through gang territory where a misstep could bring trouble raining down on their heads.

She was large, both taller and wider than Tam, and could handle herself in a fight—though probably not against an entire Exe gang. Still, she had a knife strapped to her calf, and the can of pepper spray her uncle insisted she carry everywhere. She and Tam would be all right.

But it wouldn't come to that. So far, they hadn't met any

trouble. Even though she was big, she knew how to move silently as they picked their way deeper into the Exe.

Without speaking, Tam led her down the last block before his house. They carefully skirted the broken building where the yellow-eyed smoke drifters squatted. Marny wrinkled her nose against the sickly sweet smell, glad to see Tam's place up ahead.

The house was a rickety, two-room building perched on the flat roof of an old auto-repair shop, long closed. A blue tarp gone tattered and gray flapped across part of the shelter's roof, and the walls were patched with scabby pieces of corrugated metal.

Marny followed Tam up the rickety staircase on the side of the building. The railing wobbled under her hand.

"Watch the seventh tread," Tam said. "It's pretty rotted."

Yeah, last thing he needed was for a big Samoan girl to crash through and ruin his stairs. She skipped the seventh one, then waited at the top of the landing behind Tam as he used his ring of jingling keys to open the multiple deadbolts. Old tech, but reliable. It was too easy to hack a keypad system, and the authorities didn't care if your stuff got stolen, not here in the Exe. She doubted the cops even came out this far.

Tam slipped his keys into his back pocket. A shadow moved behind the wire-webbed window next to the door. Tam held up his hand, signaling her to wait, then pushed the door open and slipped inside.

Everything was quiet for a heartbeat. Two. Marny peered through the half-open door.

"Hiiiyyaaa!" a voice screeched.

The sound was wrong, something made from an inhuman throat. The hairs on Marny's arms rose. She banged open the door, to see a small creature clinging to Tam's shoulders. Its clawed hands were tangled in his hair, and bright eyes gleamed maliciously from a pale, wizened face.

"Hey!" Tam yelled. "Get off."

He tried to shake the thing loose, but it held on tight, like some gruesome parody of a kid taking a pony ride on its dad's shoulders.

"Gotcha!" The creature laughed, showing sharp teeth.

Marny was through the door in two steps. She swept up her right arm and put some power behind it. Not quite a punch, but enough to send the oddly-jointed creature tumbling down. It flew off Tam's shoulders, its screeching laughter ending in a squawk as it landed on the carpet.

"Nice," she said, staring at the creature's bulbous, eerie-looking eyes. Its skin had a greenish tinge.

"What is this?" it hissed, glaring up at them. "Another human to see me? Sheer folly."

Tam pivoted and shut the door, snicking the locks home. "What was that about, jumping on me?"

She could see Tam's urge to kick the changeling in his face —but he'd warned her and Jennet that however the changeling was treated, the same thing would happen to the Bug. Which meant no beating up the evil faerie creature, no matter how totally deserved.

"Tee-hee. 'Twas all a bit of fun. Surprised you, did I?" The changeling grinned up at Tam and leaped to its feet. "Now feed me."

"Quite a houseguest you have there," Marny said. Maybe she shouldn't have volunteered for changeling-sitting duty after all. "As annoying as your little brother is, I prefer the Bug to *this*."

"What you think matters little to me," the changeling said.

Marny rolled her eyes at Tam and followed him into the kitchen. He flipped the electric kettle on to boil, then rummaged around in the cupboards. There didn't seem to be much to eat. Dried noodle packets, a couple lonely cans of synth-meat. Tam grabbed a few protein bars and banged the cupboard doors shut.

"Here," he said, flipping a bar through the air to the changeling.

The creature caught it and held it up to the light. "What is this item?"

"Food," Tam said, then gave Marny an exasperated look as the changeling bit into the protein bar right through the plastic packaging.

"Feh." The creature spit on the floor. "Mortal sustenance used to taste much better."

"You don't eat the wrapper," Marny said. "Peel it, like this."

She took a bar from Tam and tore off the shiny plastic. The changeling watched her, then stripped off the wrapper and popped the whole bar into his mouth.

"Still tasteless," he said, squinching his already-wrinkled face into a sour expression.

"At least we agree on that," Marny said, handing her bar to Tam.

"What?" he said. "You don't like synthesized nut-flavored protein bars?"

"I prefer my uncle Zeg's cookies."

And it was obvious Tam didn't have a lot of food in his cupboards. She wasn't hungry, and even if she were, she wouldn't eat up his few supplies.

"Me too," he said, "but I don't have any of those lying around. Tea?"

"Yeah—mint if you've got it." Tea was cheap, and it would be rude to completely refuse his hospitality.

Tam pulled out two mugs and a packet of tea bags. Marny noticed he scarfed down two of the protein bars. Right—he hadn't had any lunch. Not that school lunch was any better than the dry, non-flavored bars.

"So." She turned to the changeling, squatting on the floor like a toad. "What's your name?"

"Are you trying to trick me, mortal?" His gleaming eyes narrowed.

She raised an eyebrow. "As in…?"

"Names have power in the Realm," Tam said. "Generally, they aren't freely given out."

Marny pursed her lips. Made sense. She took the cup of tea Tam handed her.

"Right," she said. "Then what shall we call him?"

Tam frowned and shot a look at the creature. "I've been thinking of him as not-Bug."

"Catchy—but we can do better." She looked down at the fey creature again. "Changeling, what name do you use when you're in the mortal world? Doing, you know, baby impersonations."

The changeling folded its spindly arms and glared up at her. "I am called by the child's name."

"Yeah." Tam set his mug of tea on the counter. "Except we know you're not my little brother. Either you choose something, or we will."

"Yoda," Marny said, laughing internally at the idea of naming the creature after an ancient film character.

"Too obvious." Tam looked the changeling over. "How about… Bilbo."

"Nah." Marny was too fond of the Hobbit characters to give this ugly creature one of their names. "If anything, it's a Gollum."

She was glad Tam still remembered the moldering old paper book they had both read the summer they were ten. Had the author based his stories on glimpses of the Realm?

"Stop." The changeling bared his pointed teeth. "If you insist, you may call me Korrigan."

He made a mighty leap up onto the counter and took a guzzling sip of Tam's tea.

"Hey, that's mine!" Tam reached for his mug, then paused, probably thinking he didn't want to put his lips where the changeling's had just been. "Fine. Drink up."

With an evil, triumphant grin, Korrigan slurped the tea down. The thing had no manners at all. When he was done, the counter was splattered with liquid. He let out a belch that sounded like a bellowing frog, and wiped his mouth with the back of his hand. Although he seemed satisfied, Marny kept a tight hold on her own mug, just in case.

"Well, mortals," he said. "I cannot set foot over the threshold of this dwelling unless Tamlin is with me."

"And thank goodness for that," Marny muttered under her breath. Crestview sure didn't need a rude changeling creature running loose through the Exe.

Korrigan shot her a narrow-eyed look, then continued. "Since I am trapped in this wretched space, what is there to do here that will amuse me?"

"What do you normally do?" she asked.

"I squall and mewl like an infant. I flail my arms and legs, and lie in the cradle."

"Doesn't sound all that fun." In fact, it sounded stupefyingly boring.

She'd bet good credits the changeling was happy to be recognized as a faerie instead of having to pretend otherwise. Although maybe *happy* wasn't an apt word. Korrigan seemed a grumpy thing at best.

"So, you usually pretend to be much younger children," Tam said. "Why did they send you this time?"

The changeling frowned, and Marny changed her opinion from grumpy to hideously grumpy.

"It is how the thing is done," Korrigan said. "There cannot be a taking without a replacement. Most stolen children are but infants. Your brother is a special case."

That was true enough, though Marny refrained from pointing it out. Just because the Bug was all kinds of random and had tried to burn down the house a couple times didn't mean he deserved to be spirited away into the Realm of Faerie.

"Yeah," Tam said, crossing his arms. "He's a hostage."

He sounded tired and depressed, like he was about ready to give up on everything. Marny could see that losing his brother felt like the last straw.

"Tam," she said, "did you get any sleep last night?"

He shook his head in a quick, sharp negation. The shadows under his eyes were proof enough that he was exhausted.

"Go lie down," she said. "I'll show Korrigan a few basic screenie games, okay? That should keep him busy and out of trouble."

Plugging kids into screen entertainment was a time-honored tactic for keeping them occupied, and she had a feeling it would work with Korrigan. She'd guess that part of his nastiness was from sheer boredom at being marooned in the human world. Not all of his foul temper, of course. He was a fey creature from the Dark Court after all.

Yet maybe if she treated him decently, someone would do the same for the Bug.

Worry zinged through her at the thought of Tam's little brother. But they couldn't help him right now. They were doing everything they could—and for her, that meant making sure Tam got some sleep and keeping his unwelcome guest distracted and out of trouble.

"Just don't let him onto the 'net," Tam said.

"Bug's account is locked out, right?" She glanced to the corner of the living room, at Tam's netscreen setup.

She could imagine the trouble Korrigan could get into with unfettered worldwide 'net access. Not a pleasant prospect.

"Yeah," Tam said. "Log him into that, it should be fine."

He yawned, and Marny gave him a push toward the single bedroom. It was where his mom usually slept, but since she was gone...

"Get some rest," she said. "I'll introduce the changeling to the joys of Kart racing."

"Show no mercy," Tam said, heading for the bedroom.

"I won't." She grinned.

It would be fun taking the creature down a notch. And really, even if Korrigan got super cranky, she could always just sit on him.

As soon as the bedroom door closed, Korrigan began

leaping about. He bounded onto the back of the shabby couch that doubled as Tam's bed, and looked like he was going to make a leap for the light fixture.

"Chill," Marny said. "Or I won't give you any more protein bars."

"They are like eating dirt," the changeling said, but he subsided, sprawling his knobby legs out.

"You still gobbled it up quick enough." She wondered what he'd think of chocolate. Or that crazy-sweet sugar cereal the Bug liked.

On second thought, maybe hopping Korrigan up on sugar and caffeine wasn't a brilliant idea.

He made a face at her. "You see too much, mortal girl. It is not usual for a human to perceive my real form. Why, I wonder, were you able to?"

Marny went to the screen setup and flicked the power on. She could think of at least one good reason.

"I've had faerie ointment smeared around my eye," she said.

It was weeks ago, but maybe the effects were long term. Unsettling, the thought that she'd be able to see any fey folk hanging out in the human world. Not a power she was comfortable with—but it seemed like she'd have to accept it.

Korrigan shuddered. "Nasty human potion. Unfair, to see through our glamours so easily."

"Yeah, well making that potion nearly trapped my friends in the Realm forever. So I'd say it was pretty hard won."

She picked up the two gaming controllers and gave Korrigan a hard look. It was probably a good bet he'd never driven a car in his immortal life.

"Have you ever ridden on a wild beast?" she asked.

He grimaced. "Aye, the Hunt took me up and brought me to the queen, where my servitude as a changeling began. Not a ride I would wish to repeat."

Marny nodded. She'd heard the Wild Hunt once, strange and eerie over the streets of Crestview. The clear cry of a horn had floated over the barking of eldritch hounds and the thud of hoof beats racing through the sky. She was just as glad never to have seen the elfin knights on their red-eyed mounts —and especially not the horned Master of the Hunt. It was enough hearing Tam and Jennet talk about the fearsome riders.

"Okay." She studied the changeling's wrinkled face. "You've never hopped on a fox's back and steered it with its ears or anything?"

"Not if I wanted to keep my legs," Korrigan said. "The vulpine creatures of the Realm are not to be trifled with."

"Then we'll have to take this slow." Marny handed him the controller, which he immediately brought to his mouth. "Stop! It's not something you eat."

Korrigan wrinkled his nose and examined the plastic buttons. "Then what good is it?"

"Watch."

Marny booted up the kart racing game and quickly selected the easiest mode and course. She chose her favorite vehicle, the blue one with dark green stripes.

"This is my racer," she said. "I control the speed and direction here." She demonstrated the controls, pushing the buttons and levers that made her kart move.

Korrigan looked at the netscreen, then back to the hunk of plastic in its hands. "It is a magical device?"

"I guess you could say that." She supposed the mechanics

of remote-controls and screenie games were close enough to magic.

"What else might I command?" The changeling pivoted and pointed the remote at the kitchen cupboard. "Bring me a bar."

When nothing happened, he threw the controller to the floor.

"It doesn't work that way," Marny said. "You can only influence things on the screen. Which is this." She leaned forward and tapped the side of the netscreen.

"Will it produce food and drink, or fetch items from the Realm?" Korrigan asked.

"No, it just plays games. But it's fun. Now pick a kart." She pulled up the choices and used her remote as a pointer. "Do you like any of these?"

The changeling peered at the screen. "The one on the end, with the flames."

"Good pick. Now grab your controller and I'll show you how to move. Then we'll race."

Korrigan picked up the basics surprisingly quickly, and before long was zipping around the track, muttering under his breath as he tried to catch up with Marny. He screeched with glee whenever he passed one of the game-controlled racers.

"Putrid bog fungi!" he cried as his kart spun off the course yet again.

"You're taking that turn too fast," Marny said.

"My velocity matches yours," he replied, grunting as he waved the controller and got his vehicle turned back around.

"Yeah but I've got a few years of experience on you."

"But I am a fey creature, and you but a mortal girl."

"A mortal girl who's kicking your ass," she said. Still, maybe she was being too hard on him. "Do you want to try something different?"

He glanced at her, his pale eyes slitted. "Are you trying to trick me?"

"Always with the suspicion. No—I'm offering you some other options." She scrolled to a new course, featuring a race through the mushroom swamp instead of the colorful hills. "Let's do this one."

"Ah." Korrigan leaned forward, his ugly mouth splitting into a grin. "This is much more pleasant in aspect."

"All right, then." Clearly, the changeling's idea of pleasant involved copious amounts of muck and slime.

The timer counted down, and at the buzzer they took off, their bright cars zipping through the murky trees. Marny lagged a little, letting Korrigan stay close, but by the end of another hour, his skills had improved enough that she didn't need to give him a handicap. She still beat him in the overall scores, though.

"Hey." Tam opened the door of the bedroom and rubbed his eyes. "You still here, Marny?"

"Yep." She glanced out the wire-webbed window. "Getting dark."

"You're not walking home by yourself," Tam said.

"And you're not walking back alone after dropping me off," she said. "I'll ask Uncle Zeg to come get me. It's not that far." She pulled out her messager and sent her uncle a quick note.

"As if that racketing guzzler of his is low profile. I can't believe he keeps that old car running."

"We'll be okay. Zeg can out-drive anything."

"I want to race more," Korrigan said, leaping on to the

back of the couch. "Next time, I will be victorious, I am certain of it."

"You can practice against the game," Tam said. "You don't need a real person to play with."

The changeling made a face, but turned back to the netscreen and soon was accelerating through the swamp once more.

"You feeling better?" Marny asked, giving him a hard look.

The smudges beneath his eyes weren't quite as dark, and his mouth seemed less pinched with exhaustion and strain.

"Adequately," he said.

"The beta team plays tomorrow afternoon, right?" she asked.

"Yes." He ran a hand through his hair, then let the strands fall back into his face. "I hope Jennet and I can get some answers. We have to figure out how to make the game safe for normal players, instead of them getting sucked into the Realm."

"I'll come over after school again," Marny said. "Keep the freaky dude out of trouble."

"Okay. I'll get you the extra set of keys for the front door." Tam glanced at the creature squatting on the couch, and misery flashed through his eyes. "I guess that's all we can do right now."

Marny patted his shoulder. "Hang in there."

She couldn't promise that everything would come out okay—who could? But she knew they'd all try.

∾

IT WAS a sign of how upset and distracted Tam was that he didn't ask Marny how she was getting to his house that afternoon. After school, he caught a ride to the beta testing with Jennet, giving Marny a halfhearted wave as they pulled away.

She'd planned ahead, though, and arranged for her uncle to drop her off at Tam's on his way up to the VirtuMax compound. Going alone into the Exe was plain stupid.

In fact, Uncle Zeg was the only member of her family who knew she was, as she'd put it, "helping Tam with a project at his place." Her mom would freak if she knew Marny was in the Exe without Tam, and Grandma Harmony would lecture her, then insist on telling her for the thousandth time all the ways to keep the *aitu*, or ghosts, away.

Marny went up the creaky stairs to Tam's place, undid the multiple locks on the front door, then waved to Uncle Zeg. He putted away, leaving a cloud of oily smoke in the middle of the potholed street.

It was nice to be out of the house and have some breathing room, even if she had to share that room with a fey creature. Babysitting Korrigan made a nice change from the bustling, close quarters of her own home. It wasn't that much bigger than Tam's place, and felt smaller, with her younger brother's projects always underfoot, her older twin sisters arguing night and day, Dad's boisterous jokes, and Grandma Harmony's weird teas scenting the air with bitter and pungent herbs.

Marny pushed Tam's front door open. She was greeted by a swath of vines sporting bright, poisonous-looking flowers. More plants lurked in the corners, fringed with sharp teeth.

"Jump on me, and you're meat," she called as she stepped into the jungle of Tam's living room.

From overhead, Korrigan let out an unhappy sigh. He let

himself down, hand-over-hand, on one of the ropey vines hanging from the ceiling. Squatting on the floor, he blinked up at her. He almost seemed happy to have company.

"What's with the foliage?" she asked, batting away a tendril that tried to fasten around her wrist.

"This human habitation is far too plain," Korrigan said. "I thought to enliven the surroundings."

Marny kicked at a groping root. "Well, how about you un-enliven things. I'd prefer not to be some plant's snack."

"I doubt it would find you palatable," the changeling said.

Marny gave him a look, and he sniffed and waved his hands in a complex series of gestures. The vines curled up into the ceiling and the hungry-looking plants in the corner disappeared. A nearby orange flower imploded with a fleshy pop, leaving a wet spot on the dingy carpet.

"Better." Marny dug in her pack and held out a handful of silver-wrapped protein bars. "I brought you a treat."

The changeling's eyes lit, and he snatched the bars from her as if he were starving. Quickly, he stripped off the wrappers and stuffed all three bars in his mouth at once. Brown drool ran from the corner of his mouth, and Marny had to turn away from the disgusting sight. At least she'd been right that, despite his complaining, Korrigan liked the taste of the protein bars. Either that or he was really really hungry all the time.

Good thing she had another half dozen bars in her pack. Never knew when bribery would come in handy.

"Ready for some racing?" she asked.

Korrigan wiped his mouth with the back of his hand. "I shall defeat you this time."

"Yeah, we'll see about that." She was tempted to let him

win once or twice, but it felt too patronizing. The changeling was quick and clever. When he came in first, beating her, it would be on his own merits.

Marny flicked on the netscreen system, and soon she and Korrigan were jockeying for position as they sped through colorful caverns. He was getting much more skilled, she'd give him that—but he still wasn't as good as she was. They played for two hours, and she let him come in a close second a few times, to keep his spirits up.

"Okay, break time." Marny tossed the controller on the couch, then stood up and stretched.

Korrigan pouted, until she gave him another protein bar.

"So," she said. "What's it like, where you're from?"

The changeling let out a heavy sigh. For a moment the sneer fell away from his mouth.

"It is full of magic and mystery. Your mortal world is nothing but drab and weary." He flicked the brown carpet with one finger.

"You've only seen the inside of Tam's house," Marny said. "There's a lot more to discover. I bet you'd be impressed with the ocean."

"We have seas in the Realm," he said with a sniff.

Still, she suspected he'd like to get out of the tiny house at some point. Maybe she and Tam could figure out a field trip. Though she really hoped the Bug would be returned soon.

"Why don't you go back there for a quick visit, and let Tam's brother come home for a bit?" she asked.

"The queen would never allow it." Korrigan shivered, then grabbed his game controller. "Let us commence racing."

Although Marny wanted to press for more information

about the Dark Queen, she could tell Korrigan was done with that subject. For now.

They spent another hour mindlessly racing, until the rattle of the gas guzzler outside and the jingle of the locks signaled that Tam was home. He stepped through the door just as Marny scored another victory.

"Noo!" Korrigan flung down his controller.

"I win. Again." She glanced up at Tam. "Hey, how'd the beta testing go today?"

"Good." He sounded a little more upbeat. "I'll tell you about it tomorrow at school. Zeg's out there waiting for you."

"I know—the sound of his car is unmistakable." She rose and gathered up her back and coat. "See you later, Korr. Better work on those driving skills."

The changeling stuck his tongue out at her and crossed his eyes. "I shall master this ridiculous mortal game yet."

"He's totally hooked, poor guy." Marny shook her head, then headed for the door. "See you tomorrow."

She hoped whatever Tam and Jennet had managed to accomplish in-game, they were that much close to bringing the Bug home.

MARNY WAS TUCKING her things in her backpack at the end of the school day when Jennet came rushing up, her big blue eyes wide.

"We need your help," she said.

"As in?" Marny closed up her pack, then looked at Jennet. There was a pleading in her friend's expression she mistrusted.

"Um. Tam's taking Roy Lassiter to his place to see the changeling, and you have to go with them."

"What? That's a terrible idea."

Not just having to share air with Roy, but exposing Korrigan to any more people. She was starting to feel oddly protective of the ugly little guy.

"I know." Jennet pressed her lips together in the way she did when she was upset. "But we have to prove to Roy that Tam's little brother is a hostage in the Dark Realm, so he'll let me and Tam use his sim equipment to get into Feyland. The only way to do that—"

"Is to introduce him to Korrigan. I see." Marny crossed her arms. "You better hope Roy doesn't sell you and Tam out. If your dad finds out you two are spending illicit in-game time together, things could get even more severe."

"I know. But saving the Bug is more important than whether my dad grounds me for a year. Now, will you come?"

Marny let out a sigh. Of course she'd go. She picked up her backpack.

"Fine," she said. "Lead on."

She couldn't help grimacing when she saw Royal Lassiter standing outside with Tam. Ever since Roy had used his faerie glamour on her to make her play Feyland, she'd pretty much detested him. Not only had he forced her in-game despite her claustrophobia, he'd also made her have a disgusting crush on him. The boy had a very sketchy sense of decency.

Jennet gave Tam one of her *Iloveyou* smiles. "Message me when you get up to the View, and I'll meet you at Roy's. Good luck."

Roy made a noise of disgust, either at the little love darts coming out of Tam and Jennet's eyes whenever they looked at each other, or the fact that Jennet was sure he'd let them onto his sim system. Probably both.

Marny turned her shoulder to him, and stayed a couple feet behind as he led them to the parking lot where his shiny red grav-car was parked.

"I'm sitting in back," she said as Roy waved the doors open. "Tam can enjoy the pleasure of your company."

She didn't even want to brush up against him accidentally. She couldn't believe she'd once actually wanted to kiss the guy. Of course, she'd been under a spell, but still. She'd rather kiss Korrigan, who at least was honest with his bad self.

Roy slid behind the wheel and started the car.

"I don't suppose you have a real address I can put in the navbot?" he asked Tam, sounding all superior.

"Not so much." Tam's voice was calm, but Marny could see him flexing his fingers. "I'll tell you how to get there."

As they drove to the Exe, Marny braced herself against Roy's wild driving and watched the neighborhoods change. Already faded and dumpy around Crestview High, they quickly disintegrated until all pretense of normal suburbia was gone. Half the buildings were empty, and the other half, Marny didn't want to know who lived inside.

"You sure it's safe?" Roy asked, slowing to navigate over a pile of rubble in the street.

"Of course it's not," Marny said. "Just do what Tam says, and we should be all right."

She was a little worried Roy would get all bossy and make his own decisions, which couldn't end well for them. Luckily, he showed some good sense, following Tam's directions as they wound through the outskirts of the Exe.

They got to an area Marny recognized. Sure enough,

Tam's blue tarp roof came into view. He pointed to the alley beside the old auto shop.

"Pull up over there," he said. "And put the alarm on."

"Of course," Roy said. "It's triple-alarmed."

Not as alarmed as Roy would be if somebody decided to mess with his car. As if a siren would stop anyone.

"You seriously live here?" Roy asked, and Marny wanted to punch the smug expression off his face.

"Shut it," she said. "Welcome to the real world, rich boy."

Some day, she hoped Roy would get his comeuppance. Something that would shake his world, like being disowned by his rich CEO mom, or falling in love with a girl he could never have.

As soon as the car stopped, Tam slipped out and hurried up the stairs. Marny and Roy followed, though she hung back. The last thing she wanted was Roy behind her, where she couldn't see what he was up to.

Tam had the door open by the time they got to the top of the stairs. Inside, his living room was back to being a crazy jungle. Marny laughed a little, quietly. She hoped one of the flowers took a bite out of Roy's arm.

"Korrigan?" Tam called as they stepped into the house.

The smell of rank vegetation filled the air, and orange flowers with serrated teeth grew on ropey vines hanging from the ceiling. There seemed to be a waterfall in the kitchen, too. Nice touch.

"You have a way with decorating, Exie," Roy said. Beneath the bravado in his voice, she could hear fear.

He reached a finger out to touch one of the flowers, then jerked it back when the blossom opened its mouth and hissed at him.

Marny reached into her pack and pulled out a protein bar. Better to lure the changeling out than risk another ambush.

"Come out, Korr," she called. "I've got a treat for you."

The leafy canopy overhead rustled, and Korrigan stuck his head out.

"Protein bar? Give it to me." He stuck out his hand, his claws extended.

"A little less jungle, please." She held the bar out of reach and waggled it back and forth. "And ditch the carnivorous flowers."

He grimaced. "You mortals have no appreciation for the spice of danger."

Marny glared at him, and Tam let out a frustrated breath.

"We have more than enough danger going on right now," he said. Then he glanced at Roy, who looked way uncomfortable. "Seen enough?"

"Yeah." Roy swallowed, his gaze darting from Korrigan, to the flowers now smacking their lips, to the slick yellow moss under their feet.

"So, you believe us?" Tam pressed.

"Fine, fine. You were right." Roy looked up at the changeling and winced. "I guess if we can be transported to Feyland, its creatures can come out."

"You have no idea," Tam said. "Let's go."

Marny nodded. Korrigan loved an audience—maybe a little too much. As soon as the boys cleared out, she'd be able to get the changeling to clean up the jungle, and then distract him with more racing.

"One sec," Roy said, pulling out his sleek messenger. "Let me vid this."

Holding it up, he slowly turned in place, panning the

room. When he got to Korrigan, he paused and Marny could see him zooming in.

"Smile," she said to Korrigan.

The changeling obliged, grinning wide enough to show his pointed teeth. His eyes slitted nearly shut, and the proportions of his face were very clearly inhuman.

"Nice." Roy thumbed the power off and tucked his messager away.

Marny wasn't too worried that Roy would try to do anything stupid with the images, like post them out on the 'net. Stuff like that could be faked all too easily, and everyone knew it, even with someone swearing eyewitness testimony.

"No more water features in the kitchen, ok?" Tam gave the changeling a stern look.

Korrigan grimaced back, but made no promises.

Marny hid her smile. Tam should know better by now not to try to bargain with the fey folk. Even she, who had only a fraction of the experience dealing with them, knew how tricksy they could be.

"You guys go have fun," she said to Tam. "I'll make him clean up. I have the rewards, you know."

"Protein bars." Tam sounded disgusted. He was probably just jealous he hadn't figured out how fond of them the changeling actually was.

"Go," she said. "And be careful."

Despite her earlier words, Tam wasn't going to sim for fun. Tam, Jennet, and Roy were headed back into Feyland. And no matter the growing fondness Marny felt for Korrigan, she really hoped they'd be able to get Tam's brother home. Soon.

"You be careful, too," Tam said. "Keep the door fully locked."

Oh, she would. The Exe might not be full of faerie peril, but there was plenty of human danger. Everything from the fact that Tam's mom could come home at any moment, which was more complication than threat, to the packs of gangs who roamed the crumbling streets, to the yellow-eyed smoke drifters who squatted in the abandoned building down the street.

As soon as Tam and Roy left, she did up all the locks, smacking the deadbolts home and sliding the chains and bars across. Then she turned to Korrigan.

"Race?" he asked, his bulbous eyes bright.

"How about you clean up, first."

He groaned, sounding like a human teenager, but the vines curled into the ceiling and disappeared, and the waterfall slowly gurgled away down the kitchen sink drain.

"Better." Marny tossed him the second remote, then settled on the couch.

"I shall beat you this time, mortal," Korrigan said.

He tried, too. For nearly two hours they raced and zoomed, and the changeling managed to push Marny to her limit. She was hanging on to her wins, but just barely.

At last, back on the mushroom swamp course, Korrigan edged past her on a turn, and cackled.

"Prepare to lose," he said, his voice high with glee.

Marny bit her lip and pushed her speed to the max, but it was too late. With a screech of triumph, the changeling crossed the finish line a moment before her.

"Heehee!" he cried. "Victory is mine."

"Good job."

He'd worked hard for that win, and it was worth it to see the goofy grin on his ugly face. Who would have thought a faerie would enjoy playing screenie games so much?

Then his expression sobered and he lifted his head, all trace of gleefulness gone. He looked dangerous now, like the fey creature from the Dark Court he truly was.

"Someone approaches," he said, his gaze moving to the wire-webbed window.

Marny hit the pause button, cutting off the happy music tinkling from the speakers. The back of her neck prickled with unease.

"Is it Tam?" she asked, already knowing the answer.

"No." The changeling screwed up his face. "Many men, with evil intent."

Crap, and double crap. Either a gang or the drifters. She'd bet credits someone had spotted Roy's fancy red grav-car parked outside earlier, and drawn the wrong conclusions about what riches might lie inside Tam's house.

Reaching past Korr, she clicked off the lamp—a clunky brass fixture with old-fashioned wiring instead of a sensor plate. The netscreen sent a pale glow over them, the word *PAUSED* blinking like a silenced alarm. From the street below, Marny heard voices.

Then the clomp of footsteps on the stairs.

*Crash!*

She jumped at the sound of splintering wood. Somebody yelled, then cursed loudly, and she guessed they'd gone right through the rotted seventh step.

Her hand went to the knife strapped on her leg, under her jeans—but that was for closer fighting, one-on-one. It was not the right weapon to deal with a group assault.

Her heart thumping out a heavy beat in her chest, Marny slowly rose. The locks on the door would keep the intruders out. She hoped.

Korr gave her a quizzical look, and she held up her hand, signaling him to stay there.

"Hey!" The voice was accompanied by someone pounding at the door. "We know you're in there. Listen, just give us all your money, and we won't come in and hurt you."

As if Marny would crack the door open and simply hand over any nonexistent cash. Must be smoke-drifters; gang members would be more clever in their approach.

Which was good, and bad. Drifters were dumb, having numbed their brains with too much smoke. But it could also make them stupidly persistent when any normal person would go away after a while.

"I am ready to fight," Korrigan said, keeping his voice low. He flexed his clawed hands, a wild light coming into his eyes.

"I bet." He could be an asset, for sure.

But it sounded like at least a half dozen guys were outside. One group on the landing, another down in the street. The two of them against six or seven drifters wasn't good odds. Even with a scrappy fey changeling on her side.

"Come on." The banging on the door intensified. "We know you got cash."

"Begone, foul mortals," Korrigan screeched. "There is nothing here for you."

Marny sent him a sour look. Great. Although it hadn't been likely the drifters would simply leave, the chances of that happening had just evaporated to nothing.

"Some kid," one of the drifters muttered.

"Bring it up," another one said. "We'll beat the door down."

A few seconds later, the door shook with the clang of metal on metal. The drifters had found something large to bash against the door; one of those big metal burn barrels, maybe. If she and Korrigan were lucky, their attackers would only dent the door some, then go away.

But it didn't feel like a lucky night.

Clenching her hands, Marny quickly evaluated their options. She and Korrigan could retreat to the bedroom, maybe get out the window there and climb down the back of the building...

But even if she could squeeze through, the changeling wasn't able to leave the house unless Tam were with him. Dammit. They couldn't escape—so they'd have to fight.

With the constant clashing thud of the drifters at the door as a background, Marny pulled out her old messager and keyed in a quick call for help.

Not to the police—they'd take too long, if they even came out at all. Tam said the authorities ignored the Exe as much as possible. And she didn't want to risk revealing Korrigan.

*:Under attack at Tam's. Help. Bring firepower.:*

Uncle Zeg would get her message and be on the way, hopefully with the big flamethrower he'd recently finished rebuilding. Her uncle was worth at least three or four of the drifters, and she knew she could take a couple. Korrigan would pitch in, and they'd repel the attack. They just had to sit tight until Zeg showed up.

She almost messaged Tam, too, but he'd be in-game, and doubtless fighting his own battles. No, she could handle this.

Probably.

"Korr," she said, keeping her voice low, "if they break in, do you have any offensive magic to throw at them? Not the jungle though—it could get in our way."

The changeling gave her one of his horrific grins.

"I can summon any number of nasty crawlies to bite and sting our enemies, should they breach the walls," he said.

"Good. Because I have a feeling things are about to get real."

Not that she thought the drifters would smash through the door, but she'd been keeping an eye on the shadows moving across the wire-webbed living room window. One guy had what looked like a big wooden club, maybe a baseball bat, and it was only a matter of time before he started swinging it at the glass.

She bent and unplugged the cord of the old-fashioned brass lamp on the table by the couch, then stripped the shade off. In this fight, she'd rather swing something heavy at an attacker's head than try to hit a vital spot with a small, pointy object.

The yelling outside intensified, and two of the shadowy figures turned to the window. One of them lifted his club and swung.

The first crack of wood against glass made Marny wince. No telling how long the window would hold.

"Get ready," she said to Korrigan.

He flexed his spindly, oddly jointed fingers, and nodded.

Another whack, and a spider web of cracks spread across the reinforced glass. It wouldn't be long. She took a deep breath and widened her stance.

The third blow shattered the window, square-edged pieces of safety glass flying into Tam's living room.

"Ha! Told you we could bust it out." The drifter with the wooden club poked at the empty wire, then shoved it aside.

He began to clamber through the wrecked window, but Marny was ready. She brought the lamp down hard on the top of his head, and he crumpled.

"Dude. Why'd you stop?" His companion toed him in the ribs.

A second later, a swarm of weird looking insects poured from around Korrigan and out the widow. Some of them paused to bite and sting the unconscious man, but the rest kept going.

"Hey! Ow! Get off!" the man right outside the window yelled.

Marny glanced at Korrigan. He was mumbling, his fingers moving in strange patterns, his concentration on the insects.

Two more drifters tried to rush the window, which was stupid, because they couldn't both fit through. Marny whacked at them with the base of the lamp. Various cries of pain issued from outside, and one guy ran screaming down the stairs. Still, most of the drifters were not as easily gotten rid of. They'd stopped trying to bang the door down, and turned to the shattered window.

In the distance, Marny heard the loud cough and rattle of a gas car engine, and she smiled through the grimness of battle. Uncle Zeg was on his way. She and Korrigan only needed to hold their attackers off a few moments more.

The gas guzzler pulled up with a screech of brakes loud enough to make the drifters turn. Marny struck the current window-broacher on the shoulder, and Korrigan sent a particularly nasty winged scorpion at his face. The man ducked away, grimacing.

Outside the broken window, a gout of fire lit up the night, reflecting off smoke drifters' yellow-tinged eyes and casting eerie shadows over the dilapidated buildings.

"Want a taste of this?" Zeg's voice called from the street. "I'll give you three seconds to clear out of here, and then things are going to heat up."

Relief surged through Marny, and she tightened her grip on the lamp base. Her uncle was here, and the attackers were toast. Literally.

Two more drifters pelted down the stairs, reached the street, and kept running. The remaining men looked at each other.

"What now, Skeever?" one of them asked, glancing at the man who seemed to be the leader.

"We'll come back later," Skeever. "After this guy leaves."

Marny narrowed her eyes. It was actually a halfway decent plan. Uncle Zeg couldn't protect them for the entire night, after all.

Another blast of fire from the street.

"I'm running out of patience," her uncle called.

"Go." The lead drifter roughly pushed one of his men, and the rest followed.

They ran down the stairs, several of them still swatting at Korrigan's persistent pests. Welts and stings marred their faces and hands, and Marny hoped the bugs had gotten under their clothes, too.

Now that their enemies were fleeing, the adrenaline that had powered her faded, leaving a shaky sadness in its wake.

Tam's house wasn't safe anymore, and her heart wrenched at all the losses he'd been facing. His mom taking off again. His brother stolen by the faeries. And now this.

Uncle Zeg waited until the last drifter ran away into the dark, then, still carrying his flamethrower, slowly backed up the stairs. Marny didn't warn him about the missing seventh stair—she didn't need to. For a big man, her uncle was amazingly light on his feet, and constantly aware of his surroundings. He was pretty much her hero.

Without even looking behind him, he took a giant step backward over the gaping hole.

"You okay up there?" he called softly to them.

"Yeah," Marny said. "Nice timing."

He smiled, teeth white in the dark bush of his beard. "I try."

"Korr, make sure your creatures don't attack my uncle," Marny said.

"They have already returned home," the changeling said.

She didn't ask where home was. Probably some poisonous forest in the heart of the Realm.

"Letting me in?" Uncle Zeg asked from the dented-in door.

Marny set the lamp down, her hand stiff from clutching the brass base. She snapped on the kitchen light, then went and undid the locks. The metal door opened fine. Too bad the window was wrecked.

Her uncle stood a minute, just looking at her, then set his flamethrower down and enveloped her in a big bear hug. Not many people could do that. She buried her face in his shoulder, smelling smoke and gas fumes.

"Glad you're all right," he said, his voice vibrating through her.

Two wobbly breaths, and she was better.

"Yeah," she said, stepping away. "We're good. Uncle Zeg, meet Korrigan."

She gestured to where the changeling crouched, his bulbous eyes gleaming.

"Charmed," Uncle Zeg said with a nod. He actually meant it, too.

Korrigan blinked, then smiled. "Likewise, mortal man."

As soon as her uncle stepped inside, Marny did up all the locks again.

"I'm letting Tam know what happened," Uncle Zeg said, pulling out his messager.

"Good idea."

She was happy to let her uncle send the message. Her fingers still felt numb from the fight. Plus, she felt too sorry for Tam at the moment for her words to come out right. He didn't need, or want, her sympathy. Life happened, and sometimes you ended on the bottom of the pile. Pity from friends only made it worse.

"He and Roy are on their way," Uncle Zeg said.

"Good." Marny set her hands on her hips and studied the smashed-out window. "He'll have to move out—at least for a while."

"Yep. Drifters'll be back, and more vicious than ever."

"Good thing your flame thrower works," Marny said.

"Well…" Her uncle's smile was a little sheepish. "The flame part works great. The thrower mechanism leaves a little bit to be desired."

"What? You mean you couldn't have shot fire at the drifters?" She didn't know whether to laugh or cry.

Korrigan nodded in approval. "A show of force is often more impressive than the actuality."

"Then why the crawlies?" Marny asked the changeling. "Why not a big ogre or something?"

"I have no dominion over those kind," Korrigan said. "And I have no desire to be trampled flat beneath enormous feet."

"Fair enough."

"Your insects seemed quite effective," Uncle Zeg said. "From what little I could see."

It was true. Korrigan had come through for them in the fight, in his own peculiar way.

The changeling lifted his head and sniffed the air.

"Tam Linn arrives," he said.

Marny blew out a breath, letting the ache of pity go along with it. Tam would deal, as he always dealt.

She heard his light steps on the creaky stairs, his pause when he saw the broken-out tread, then his quick rush up to the door.

"Guys?" He tapped on the metal. "It's me, Tam."

Zeg undid the locks and opened the door. Tam stepped in, his expression grim, and Marny decided a big, enveloping hug was the best tactic. After all, it had worked for her.

"Tam," she said, letting go when she felt he was ready.

"Good to see you're ok," he said. "What happened?"

"A couple hours after you and Roy left, we heard someone coming up the stairs. The smoke drifters. They said if we gave them money, they'd go away." She grimaced at the door. "Then they tried to batter down the door."

"We fought them," Korrigan added eagerly. "Mistress Marny laid about with her club, while I sent poisonous crawlies to bite and torment."

"Club?" Tam glanced about, looking for her weapon.

"Yeah," Marny said, pointing her thumb at the lamp. "One guy started coming through the window, so I bashed him.

Between that and Korr's bugs, we drove them off. With a little help from Uncle Zeg."

She could see the guilt in Tam's eyes. But it wasn't his fault.

"They haven't come back?" he asked.

"Yet." Uncle Zeg picked up his flame thrower. "But they will. Grab anything important, Tam, anything you want to keep for good. We're clearing you out of here."

For an instant Tam looked lost. "This is my home. I can't just leave."

Marny squeezed his shoulder.

"Where's Roy?" Uncle Zeg asked.

"Waiting with the car," Tam said.

"Now that you are here and can accompany me, we may depart," Korrigan said, oblivious to the undercurrents. He scrambled into the kitchen, hopped onto the counter, and began taking protein bars from the cupboard. "We must take all these. And the screenie system."

Marny felt a wry smile twist her lips. The changeling had his priorities clear, for sure.

"Tam," she said. "It's not secure here anymore." She hated the look in his eyes, but he had to come to grips with the fact his home wasn't a sanctuary any longer.

"But, what if my mom..." He swallowed hard, then continued. "What will Mom think, when she comes home?"

"Leave her a note, and hope the drifters don't mess with it?" There weren't any good solutions.

"You can't stay here." Zeg unplugged the netscreen and began winding up the cords. "I'll take the system down. You go get your stuff."

Tam turned, moving like he was underwater, and started

gathering things up—his clothes, a couple books, a battered teddy bear.

He stood there for a moment, arms full of his possessions.

"Here." Marny grabbed one of the blankets off the couch and spread it out, then took the teddy bear and set it in the middle. "Anything from the bedroom?"

"Yeah." He blinked, clearly trying to focus. "Picture album, jewelry box."

"Go get them."

Tam laid the possessions on the blanket, then headed for the bedroom.

"I'll take this lot to the car," Zeg said, arms full of the netscreen setup.

"Good," Marny said.

The sooner they got out of there, the better. She undid the locks for her uncle, then turned back to the living room. Korr was still rummaging around in the kitchen, filling a plastic bag with protein bars and anything else that caught his eye.

Tam came back out of the bedroom, carrying a few small items and a green dress that probably was his mom's favorite. Wordlessly, he added them to the pile on the blanket, and Marny twisted it up into a bundle.

Uncle Zeg bounded up the stairs and into the living room, his hair wild and frizzy.

"Hurry," he said. "There's something happening at the end of the street."

Probably the smoke drifters gathering. Marny gave Tam a hard look. Whether he was ready or not, they had to go.

Korrigan hopped down from the counter, dragging the plastic bag behind him.

"Let us away," he said, sounding like this was the best adventure ever.

Which, considering he now got to leave the tiny house and see more of the mortal world, it probably was.

"Anything else?" Marny hefted the bundled blanket over her shoulder.

"No," Tam said. "Wait—there's a brand new Zing sim system downstairs."

Uncle Zeg shook his head. "Hopefully the drifters won't think of the shop—or be able to break in. We'll come get it tomorrow."

"Once we repair the window, we can bring everything back," Tam said.

Marny wasn't so sure. The drifters were persistent, and dangerous. It would take more than a few days for them to calm down and slide back into their smoke dreams. Weeks, maybe. And where would Tam live in the meantime?

"Come, come," Korrigan called impatiently.

Through the open door, Marny could hear the rumble of voices borne on the chilly air.

"Marny, ride with me," Uncle Zeg said, starting down the stairs. "Tam, you and the changeling go with Roy."

"But—" Tam started to protest.

"Git 'im!" a rough voice cried from the street. "They're taking the loot!"

"GO!" Zeg shouted, pulling Marny with him down the stairs.

She leaped over the broken tread, and at the bottom of the stairs glanced back at Korrigan. She didn't like to leave him, but he'd be all right with Tam.

"Quick," her uncle said.

Down the block, the drifters were coming toward them, carrying torches. Looked like Uncle Zeg's flamethrower had given them some unfortunate ideas.

"Hey," Roy stuck his head out the window of his grav-car, parked right behind Zeg's guzzler. "What's going on?"

He shot a glance at the approaching drifters, and went pale.

"Start the car," Tam called, clearing the last step.

Marny was glad to see Korrigan right beside him. She sprinted to Uncle Zeg's vehicle and wrenched the passenger door open. It screeched loudly, and the lead drifter, Skeever, lifted his head, his crazed eyes fixing on Marny.

"Over there, ijidts!" he yelled, shaking his torch toward the cars.

The drifters surged forward, their torches leaving oily smears of light against the darkness.

"Get in," Uncle Zeg said, then whirled. "All of you, go!"

"Tam, hurry!" Roy yelled, sliding the passenger-side door open.

Marny buckled in, her fingers clumsy with fear. The drifters were almost on them, dammit. Why was Tam just standing there, staring down the street with that look on his face?

He turned to Uncle Zeg, expression tight with anxiety. And hope.

"My mom's out there," he said. "I have to get her."

Uncle Zeg paused, halfway in the car. "I'll help."

"No. Get Marny out of here. Meet us by The View."

Tam and his drastic heroics. She scowled at him and started to unbuckle her seatbelt.

"Young lady, you stay put," her uncle warned.

He glanced down the street, then, with a low curse, threw himself into the driver's seat and slammed the door. The guzzler started with a coughing roar, and he accelerated forward. The drifters started yelling. One of them grabbed a chunk of concrete from the street and flung it at Roy's car. It left a dent in the shiny red finish.

"We can't just leave Tam," Marny said to her uncle.

"We're not."

Uncle Zeg spun the wheel until they faced back toward the drifters. He thumbed on the high beams, and the mob halted, squinting. Tam picked up Korrigan and threw him into the back of Roy's car, the bag of protein bars clutched to his chest.

The leader of the drifters lunged and grabbed Tam's arm as he got into the grav-car.

"No!" Marny cried.

Uncle Zeg gunned the engine and the guzzler shot forward, but Skeever was already collapsing on the ground. She didn't know what Tam had done, but it had been effective.

Roy's car roared to life, and he skidded around into a U-turn. Sudden alarms and flashing lights split the air, and the drifters milled, confused.

"Roy's car alarm," Uncle Zeg said. "Good move. Now hold on—we're out of here."

"But Tam's mom..."

She watched, heart thumping in her throat, as the grav-car reached a slight figure in a yellow coat. Tam reached out and pulled her into the vehicle.

"They got her. And they'll catch up."

The night cracked again, this time with the sound of a gunshot.

Uncle Zeg accelerated hard, leaving the scorch of burning rubber behind. Marny swiveled in the seat, checking to make sure the red car was behind them.

A searing flash of light made her wince and blink. Then came a chest-rattling *whump* as Tam's house went up in flames. The blue tarp on the roof melted and curled from the gasoline-fueled fire racing over the building. The drifters had brought Molotov cocktails.

And now Tam really had no home to return to. Her eyes burned with smoke, with tears.

Once they got out of the Exe, Uncle Zeg drove quietly, taking the streets that led to The View. Halfway up the final winding road to the compound, he pulled over and killed the engine. The silence of the night pressed in around them.

"So," Uncle Zeg said. "Tell me about the weird creature."

He'd been remarkably calm about encountering Korrigan —but then, he wasn't ruffled by much. And they'd had more pressing issues at the time, like dealing with the smoke drifters.

"That's Korrigan," she said. "Tam's brother was stolen by the faeries, and they left a changeling in his place."

"And you ended up as his babysitter?"

"Someone had to watch the little guy while Tam's in-game."

Uncle Zeg turned in the seat to look at her.

"You didn't feel like mentioning any of this to me?"

Marny shifted with discomfort. "Tell you that faeries are real? Would you have believed it?"

"Yes." His voice was clear with honesty.

"I'm sorry. But everything's been happening so fast." She let out a breath.

"Tam and Jennet's odd character disappearances in the Feyland beta testing aren't just glitches, are they?" he asked.

"No."

She didn't say any more. The fact that Tam and Jennet were entering the Realm was their secret to spill.

Uncle Zeg tapped his fingers on the wheel. "I won't press you, though I suspect tonight will provide some answers."

"What's Tam going to do?" She could voice her worry to Uncle Zeg. "His house is toast—literally."

At least he had his mom, and a few of their most prized possessions.

Uncle Zeg scratched his beard. "The apartment behind my place has been empty since Grandma Tina passed."

"You know Tam won't take charity."

"It's not charity if he works for it. The place needs cleaning up. And he could do some jobs for me at the simcafe too. Don't worry, I'll make it comfortable for him to accept."

Marny nodded with relief. Tam and his family had a place to go. He might be too stubborn to agree on his own behalf, but he'd do it for his mom and the Bug. Provided they got the kid safely out of the Dark Court. Her stomach tightened with worry. What if they couldn't? Tam's life was dire enough without that fear hanging over them like a tornado poised to strike.

Her uncle glanced in the rearview mirror. "Here comes Royal."

Headlights illuminated the inside of the car as Roy pulled up behind them. Marny opened the passenger door, wincing as it squeaked again. She grabbed the blanket filled with Tam's stuff.

The door of Roy's grav-car slid open.

"Special View taxi at your service," Roy said, getting out and waving to the back seat. "Everybody in. We all need to go to Spark's."

"I figured something along those lines," Uncle Zeg said, clambering into the back. "I'm sure the gate guards wouldn't let my car through this time of night."

Tam was in the front seat, his mom on his lap. She looked small and fragile, her gaze unfocused as though she wasn't seeing at the real world at all, but some dream inside her head.

Marny put Tam's bundle on the floor, picked up Korr, and then squeezed in beside Zeg.

"Crowded in here," she said. "And no, Korr, you can't sit on my lap."

He made a face, but didn't protest as she set him down in the middle of the backseat floor. There wasn't much room there, between the bundle, her legs, and Uncle Zeg's, but the changeling would be well hidden from curious humans. Like the guards at the gate.

"We'll be at Spark's in a minute," Roy said, getting back in the car. "Sit tight."

"Like we have any other choice," Marny said.

At least wedged in like this, they wouldn't go flying when Roy took the turns too fast.

The grav-car slid under the plas-metal arch of the view, the guards waving them past without a second glance. Guess the CEO's son could zip in and out any time he liked.

Marny stared at the perfectly landscaped lawns and large houses. The View was so artificial looking. Nobody real lived that way—no toys in the yards, no weeds in the lawn, no character or color anywhere.

"What's the plan?" she asked Tam.

He turned his head, one arm still cradled protectively around his mom. "The beta team has to go in-game to rescue my brother. Tonight. We were going to use the vid Roy made of Korrigan to convince everyone, but..." He shrugged.

"Nothing better than the actual creature," Marny said.

She patted Korrigan on the shoulder. The shape of his bones felt strange under her hand.

It had been a wild night, and was getting wilder. She was thankful she didn't have to sim into Feyland with the team. There were enough of them that she wouldn't have to force herself onto a sim system—though if she really had to, she would. The thought made her shudder, and she distracted herself by counting up the beta-testing team in her mind: Tam, Jennet, Roy, Uncle Zeg, sim-star Spark Jaxley, and...

"Are you seriously going to ask Jennet's dad to come with you?" she asked.

"We have to." Tam didn't sound happy about it. "We need everyone. And Jennet has been trying to tell him about Feyland for months now. Maybe he'll finally believe her."

Marny hadn't met the man, but he seemed rigid in his opinions.

Then again, they had Korrigan.

"Here we are," Roy said, pulling up to an enormous mansion.

The place rose into the night, at least four stories of glass and steel. Behind the building, the lights of Crestview were spread out like a twinkling blanket. Marny looked, finding the smudge where the Exe glowed with a few sullen lights.

They all piled out of Roy's car, Tam carefully leading his mom, while Korrigan scampered out. For a second, Marny thought the changeling was going to throw himself on the lawn and roll around like a dog, but he managed to restrain himself.

"Okay, everyone—behave." Roy said.

Marny suspected he was mostly talking to Korrigan. And maybe Zeg, who liked to mess with authority. She sent her uncle a half smile, which he returned. No matter how crazy or stressful, this was a prime adventure.

The huge front door swung open at their approach. Probably cameras and sensors all over the place, up here at the top of the compound. A blank-faced security guard stood sentry, and behind him Marny glimpsed a warmly-lit entryway and spacious hall.

"Hi," Roy said. "We'd like to see Spark."

"I'll inform Miss Jaxley you're here," the guard said. "Wait in the great room."

He flicked his gaze to Korrigan, and though his expression didn't change, Marny saw the flicker in his eyes. She hoped Spark's people were discreet.

Roy beckoned them all in, then led the way down the hall, clearly comfortable with the mansion's layout. They passed a table holding a vase full of white lilies, their sweet smell perfuming the air.

What a crazy parade they were. Arrogant gamer boy up front, Tam and his totally spaced-out mom next, Marny after them, trying to keep Korrigan from darting into the side rooms, and Uncle Zeg in the back, big and fuzzy.

The great room was, well, huge. Two-story windows on the far wall looked out over Crestview, the orange city glow washing out the sky above until only a few stars showed through. Tam steered his mom to one of the tan couches at the side of the room. She sat, staring out the window, and

Marny hoped she wasn't completely lost. Surely she was inside there, somewhere, and would wake up soon.

Uncle Zeg stood by the door, and Marny took her place beside him. Neither of them wanted to make themselves comfortable. Not until they knew what was going on, and where they fit in.

Roy grinned at Korrigan. "Take a seat," he said, pointing to the big couch in the center of the room.

Obviously he wanted the changeling to make an impression the second Spark walked in.

Korrigan gave him a toothy smile, then hopped up and squatted on the plush upholstery. He looked wild and matted and dangerous, incongruous in the middle of the fancy mortal trappings. Give him a carnivorous forest, or a treacherous stream, and he'd be right at home.

Did he miss the Realm? It was hard to tell, he was such an irascible creature, but Marny thought maybe he did, despite the lure of protein bars. Certainly he didn't belong in the human world.

Brisk footsteps approached, and Spark Jaxley appeared at the door. In person, she looked just as prime as the gaming posters featuring her image—same bright magenta hair, same intent, intelligent gaze.

She paused and raised one eyebrow when she saw them all gathered in the room. Then her gaze found Korrigan, and the other brow rose.

"Well," she said. "This is interesting."

The changeling stood, his clawed feet gripping the couch, and made her a bow.

"Well met, milady," he said in his scratchy voice.

"I take it you're not from around here," Spark said.

Marny pursed her lips in approval of the gamer girl's calm reaction.

"He's from Feyland," Tam said. "I know it's hard to believe, but the game connects our world to the Realm of Faerie. Which, as you can see, is real."

Spark's mouth firmed, her eyes narrowed in thought. "There have been some strange things in that game, I'll admit. Things not even prime-level programming could achieve. So does this mean that faeries are overrunning the earth? Should we be freaking out?"

"Not yet," Tam said. "But things might get dire."

Zeg leaned forward, absorbing Tam's words.

"What are we going to do about it?" Uncle Zeg asked. "I presume the beta team is going in-game. Then what?"

"Then we hope we get lucky," Roy said, a twinge of bitterness in his voice. "Tam and Jennet have apparently managed to score an epic sword and talk to the guardians between the realms, or something like that."

Tam gave Roy a serious look. "It wasn't all fun and games."

"Speaking of Jennet," Spark glanced around, "where is she?"

Spark slowly walked around the couch, keeping an eye on Korrigan, and then leaned against the back. Marny moved into the room, too. No point in standing around awkwardly, now that it was clear Spark wasn't going to throw them out.

"Jennet should be on her way over," Tam said. "With her dad."

"Her dad?" The surprise was clear in Spark's voice.

"There's no other way for us to get into VirtuMax headquarters and onto the sim systems," Tam said. "We need Mr. Carter's help—and his access codes."

"Like Zeg said, then what?" Spark asked.

"We'll make a plan," Tam said. "As soon as they get here."

"We're here," Jennet said from the doorway.

She glanced at Korrigan still crouching on the plush tan couch, then swallowed and looked back at her dad. Marny mentally crossed her fingers. She'd never met Jennet's dad, but his actions spoke plenty loud.

"What the hell is that?" Mr. Carter stopped, one foot over the threshold. His expression was a mixture of confusion and revulsion as he stared at the changeling.

Marny studied Korrigan. She'd gotten used to, and a little fond of, his bulbous eyes, the slash of his mouth filled with sharp teeth, and the unlikely arrangement of his limbs. But he was still a revolting, otherworldly creature.

"That," Tam said, "is a changeling from the Unseelie Court of the Realm of Faerie."

"I…" Jennet's dad blinked, clearly having problems processing what he was seeing.

Uncle Zeg stepped forward, his voice sympathetic. "Hard to take in, I know. I've seen a lot of things in my life, but this is one of the strangest."

"Is it real?" Mr. Carter took a few hesitant steps into the room.

Korrigan narrowed his eyes, unhappy that his existence was in doubt.

"Shall I conjure up my crawlies, the better to convince you?" he asked crankily.

"No need," Marny said quickly, shaking her head. "You're proof enough, Korr. Plus, your bugs are hideous."

If Jennet's dad saw the weird nightmarish creatures, he'd

probably run screaming out the door. Better to take things slowly for now.

"Can I... touch it?" Mr. Carter asked.

He approached the changeling, one hand out. Marny wanted to warn him it was a bad idea; but then again, letting Korr be himself was the best way to convince Jennet's dad of his reality.

With a hiss, the changeling swiped his thick black claws out, catching the sleeve of Mr. Carter's jacket. Korrigan pulled, and Jennet's dad stumbled over to stand face-to-face with the faerie. The rasp of Mr. Carter's breathing was loud in the watching silence.

"Close enough, mortal?" Korrigan bared his teeth.

"Let him go." Marny stepped up, ready to interfere if things got nasty.

It was one thing to prove he was real, but there was a line she couldn't allow Korr to cross. No injuries. Either to fey creatures or human allies.

The changeling grimaced unhappily, but pulled his claws free and released Jennet's dad. Mr. Carter took three hasty steps back. His face was pale, and a drop of sweat trickled down from his temple.

"All right," he said, pulling down the sleeve of his jacket. "I believe you."

About time, too.

"Finally," Tam said, echoing Marny's thoughts.

Jennet's dad studied Korrigan a moment longer, then rubbed his face.

"I owe you an apology," he said, turning to where Jennet stood beside Tam. "To both of you. Honey, I... you have to understand how impossible your stories sounded, I thought you were making up wild excuses."

Jennet crossed her arms, a stubborn look on her face, and Marny didn't blame her. A single apology wouldn't erase months of issues.

"This would have been a lot simpler if you'd believed me in the first place," she said.

"I know." To his credit, Mr. Carter sounded genuinely sorry.

"Hey." Uncle Zeg, always the peacemaker, clapped his hand on Mr. Carter's shoulder. "We all make mistakes. The thing is to keep moving forward. Speaking of which, it's getting late, and we have plans to make."

From what Marny had gathered about the beta testing, the two adults had spent some time questing together. They seemed an unlikely pair, but then again, stranger things had happened.

She glanced at Korrigan. He still looked grumpy. With a wink, she tossed him one of the foil-wrapped protein bars she'd grabbed from his stash.

Although he scowled at her, he deftly caught it.

"Zeg's right," Spark said. "Everybody, sit down. We need to sort things out."

Roy, of course, immediately sprawled in the most comfortable-looking chair. "I'm thinking we wait until after midnight to sneak into headquarters, in case anyone's working late."

Tam and Jennet moved to the small sofa, and Marny settled into one of the double-wide armchairs. Uncle Zeg followed her lead. Nobody sat next to Korrigan.

"I'll ask the cook to throw together some pizzas," Spark said. "No commando raids on an empty stomach."

Marny agreed. When was the last time she had eaten? Or Tam, for that matter—the boy was always hungry.

"Ok." Tam leaned forward, resting his elbows on his knees. "You've all met Korrigan. He's the changeling that..." He glanced over at his mom, who seemed entranced by the lights of Crestview sparkling below.

Tam swallowed, then continued. "The changeling that was left in place of my brother."

"I don't understand," Mr. Carter said.

"Dad," Jennet said, "the Dark Court faeries stole Tam's little brother and are keeping him hostage. Our job tonight is to rescue him."

"Let me see if I have this right," Uncle Zeg said. "The game of Feyland actually leads to fairyland—which is a real, magical place?"

Marny knew that her uncle understood—he'd gotten it right away. But clearly Mr. Carter was still a little lost. Didn't hurt to restate things for his benefit. Especially since they needed him on their side in order to enter VirtuMax's super-secure headquarters and log on to the beta-test sim systems.

"Yes," Tam said.

"That'll be something to see." Her uncle's brown eyes gleamed with interest. "So, we go in-game, find this Dark Court place, and rescue Tam's little brother."

"Except it won't be that easy," Roy said, showing a rare flash of good sense.

Spark nodded. "I assume we're in for an epic battle."

"Yeah." There was the bare edge of worry in Tam's voice.

"Thing is, there are two courts, and apparently they've joined forces."

"So this is a bad thing?" Zeg asked.

"Extremely." Tam sat up straight. "Which is why we need everyone's help. Jennet and I can't defeat the king and queen, not by ourselves."

Roy made a noise, and Tam shot him a look. "Not the three of us either, Roy. You don't know what the Dark Queen is like."

Marny knew that Tam and Jennet, working together, had barely beaten the Dark Queen in battle once before. And that, with the addition of Roy, they'd managed to escape the Bright King's court. But Tam was right—if the two fey monarchs were working together, the humans would need all the help they could get.

AFTER CONSUMING the better part of five pizzas, the beta team had their plan of attack. Two plans, really. The first involved sneaking into VirtuMax, and the second was how to proceed in-game once they were in Feyland.

Marny didn't say much, just munched her olive and pepperoni slice and kept an eye on Korrigan. He seemed partial to the all-veggie pizza, which surprised her a little. Then again, she didn't really want to know what his idea of a gourmet meal was. Worms and dirt, probably. Raw fish.

Tam was feeding his mom pieces of cheese pizza. She was still in a daze, but maybe the food would help. Marny went to join him on the side couch.

"What's your mom's first name?" she asked.

It was obvious to her, if not everyone else, that she'd be staying at Spark's to look after Korrigan and Tam's mom. But if something went wacky, she wasn't sure the woman would answer to "Mrs. Linn." And definitely not to "hey, Tam's mom!"

"It's Lara," Tam said, a little catch in his voice.

Jennet laid her hand on his knee. "She'll be all right."

"Maybe." Tam took his mom's unresisting hand and turned it, holding her wrist to the light. "Do you see that?"

Marny squinted and leaned forward. Despite her fear she'd be looking at drug-related marks, the only thing on Lara's skin was a pattern of silvery dots. Almost like...

"A faerie handprint?" Jennet asked.

"Yeah. My mom said a 'shining girl' talked to her tonight, and told her to come home. I don't know if it was a malicious faerie, or one trying to help." He shivered.

"Good thing you got her out of there," Marny said. "Before—"

She made herself stop. The last thing Tam needed was a reminder that his home was now a burned-out shell.

"Okay!" Spark called, standing up and stretching her hands. "Are we ready to do this?"

Jennet glanced at her dad, who had set aside his half-eaten slice of Canadian bacon and pineapple. He nodded and stood.

"I suppose so," he said.

Tam rose, his worried gaze focused on his mom. "Stay here with Marny," he said. "I'll be back in a while."

His mom smiled at him, her expression still dreamy and unfocused. It was hard to know if she even understood what he was saying.

"Take care of her," he said to Marny. It was more a plea than a command.

"No worries," she said.

That was her, Marny Fanalua; babysitter to changeling creatures and zoned-out moms. Still, it was better than squeezing into a sim chair and enclosing herself in the stifling helmet. Even the thought of it made her throat scratchy with rising panic. Nope, small spaces and her didn't get along at all.

"Ready?" Uncle Zeg asked in his calm, rumbling voice.

For a half second, Marny wanted to jump up and grab his arm, beg him not to put himself and her friends in danger. But they had to go. It was what heroes did.

The rest of the beta team nodded and started moving to the door.

"Good luck," Marny said. "I'll keep an eye on things here."

Tam turned and pointed at Korrigan. "Stay in this building, and do what Marny tells you."

Marny raised her brows. The changeling would certainly do the first, and definitely not the second. But that was okay —she had a few more protein bars in her pocket.

Spark gave her tight smile. "If you need anything, ask my staff. I've told them you have the run of the place."

"We'll probably just hang out in this room," Marny said. She didn't want to go chasing Korrigan through a five-story mansion.

"There's a vidscreen on the left wall. The painting slides down and the controls are there." Spark pointed. "And tell the house if you want something sent up from the kitchen."

"Will do. Now go kick some faerie butt," Marny said. Korrigan squawked, and she sent him an exasperated look. "Present company excepted, of course."

Uncle Zeg gave her a big hug, and Jennet a more diminutive one. Tam squeezed her shoulder and she squeezed his in return, Roy sent her a jaunty salute, Spark waved, and Mr. Carter just looked stressed.

Then they were gone, trooping down the hall and out into the chilly night. The big mansion seemed way too quiet. Marny tried to ignore the little flare of jealousy that all her friends were going off to fight while she remained on babysitting duty. Epic battles were their thing, not hers.

*Don't you think you're good enough? a voice inside her whispered. You're a better gamer than Roy. A better person.*

Yeah, well. She might be both those things, but she was still plain old Marny. Not a brilliant gamer like Tam, or a brave rich-girl like Jennet. Not even a CEO's spoiled kid. Just an ordinary girl, who took up a little extra space in the world.

She let out a breath, then stepped back into the room and closed the door. It might be a "great room," but compared to the enormous expanse of the rest of the house, it felt downright cozy

Korrigan was rooting around in the leftover pizza. Tomato sauce made his claws look bloody.

"Are you done eating?" Marny asked.

"There is no more of the delicious kind left." The changeling frowned.

"Then let's get you cleaned up."

There was a lavish bathroom attached to the great room, of course. There was probably a bathroom for every room in the place. Before taking Korrigan in, she glanced at Tam's mom, but Lara seemed fine, caught up in some reverie only she could see.

"What is this?" Korrigan hopped into the big bathtub, then rapped on the sides. "A bin to put treasure in?"

"No. You fill it with water to bathe in. Like a little pond. And before you ask, I'm not running you a bath." Seeing Korrigan without his tunic and trousers would probably scar her for life.

He didn't press the point, which was good, though he did splash water from the sink all over the floor. Marny mopped it up with one of the thick cream-colored towels. The smell of floral soap perfumed the air.

When they went back into the other room, Marny was relieved to see that Lara hadn't moved.

"Let us kart race," Korrigan said, scrambling up to the back of the couch and giving Marny a hopeful look.

"I don't think there's a screenie system in here," Marny said.

"Then find one," the changeling demanded.

Marny shook her head. She wasn't going to impose on Spark's hospitality. And she had a feeling that asking the staff to accommodate a grumpy fey creature like Korrigan and get him set up for gaming would be too much.

"We can watch some vids, though," she said, heading over to the wall.

The control panel was right where Spark had said. Marny hit the button to activate the vidscreen, and the image of a newscaster appeared. Boring. She scrolled through the channels.

"See anything you like?" she asked.

"Yes! There." Korrigan pointed to the channel where a lion chased gazelles over the dry African plains.

They probably didn't have lions in the Realm of Faerie, but

if they did, she could imagine Korrigan trying to take one down. Or tame it. The thought made her smile.

Once she got the changeling settled in front of the screen, she went over to Tam's mom. Maybe some contact with the real world would help her come back from whatever dreamland she seemed to be inhabiting.

"Hey, Lara." Marny sat down beside Tams' mom, who didn't turn her gaze from the window. "What are you looking at?"

"All the pretty lights. And wings," Lara said softly, rubbing the silver marks on her wrist.

Marny leaned forward and peered out the window. It was hard to see past the flickering reflection of carnage on the savannah.

There—a flicker of gossamer wings. A scattering of sparks moving through the sky.

"Um, Korr?" Marny said. "Do you see anything interesting outside?"

The changeling glanced out the window, then shrugged. "Only the pixies and faerie maids."

She swallowed. "You mean creatures from the Realm are flying around out there?"

"They are boring, insipid creatures," Korrigan said. "Lions are of far more interest."

"To you, maybe." Marny stood and moved to the window, letting her shadow cut the light from the room so she could see out more clearly. "Why are they there?"

"The boundary between the worlds is thinning," the changeling said. "I can feel the fey magic seeping out."

"Is this because of the beta team going in-game?"

"Perchance. Or because, with my presence in your world

and the mortal boy's in the Dark Court, the connection here is strong. This city is becoming a nexus, where the two worlds may more easily overlap."

She didn't like the sound of that.

From the darkness outside, a faerie maiden suddenly swooped close to the glass. She was about as tall as Marny, but thin as a handful of sticks. Pale wings protruded from her back, flapping slowly. As they caught the light they shimmered, opalescent. Tam's mom let out a sigh.

"So pretty," she said.

Yeah, until you looked closely and saw the sharp teeth, the alien consciousness in those pupil-less eyes. Marny shivered. The team better rescue Tam's brother, and help stop whatever was letting fey creatures through into their world.

"Do we have to worry about anything dangerous getting loose?" Marny asked.

She made shooing motions at the faerie, but the creature hovered in place outside the window, staring at her. Creepy.

"Unlikely," Korrigan said over the cries of dying gazelles. "The gateway is not big enough to allow more than the lesser fey folk through."

"Let's hope that doesn't change." She squeezed her hands into fists. The beta team had better succeed.

Fewer things were worse than waiting around, powerless. The next few hours were going to crawl by.

"Gah!" Korrigan's strangled call made Marny turn.

He was lying on the plush carpet, pinned there by two small, squat creatures even uglier than he was. One of them raised a sharpened wooden spear.

"Stop!" Marny yelled.

Adrenaline jolting through her, she bent and whipped out

her knife, then dashed around the couch and shoved Korrigan's attacker away. The blade touched the creature's leathery skin, and it hissed in pain and retreated a few steps.

"Get off him," she warned, waving her knife at the one still holding Korrigan down.

It scowled at her, eyes full of malice, and slowly released the changeling. Korrigan scuttled back on all fours, then stopped and raised his hands.

"Begone, foul hobgoblins," he screeched. "Before I drive you forth with stings and bites."

The one holding the spear growled and shook it at Korrigan, but Marny put herself between it and the changeling.

"You heard him." She pointed her knife at the hobgoblins. "Or do you need more convincing?"

With a last, evil glare, the creatures muttered something that might have been a spell. Purple light flared, and Marny put up her arm to shield her eyes. When she lowered it, there was no sign of the hobgoblins. Her heart was pounding, the beat a steady thump, thump in her ears.

"Are they really gone?" She turned to Korrigan.

"Aye." He winced. "Kindly put away your blade, Mistress Marny. The cold iron burns the air."

"Right. Sorry."

She remembered Jennet telling her that the fey folk couldn't abide the touch of iron. Another good reason to carry her knife, evidently.

Marny glanced at where Tam's mom sat. The woman seemed oblivious to what had just happened, and was still staring out the window. At least the freaky faerie maiden was gone.

Korrigan let out a grunt and got to his feet.

"Are you okay?" Marny slid her knife back in her leg sheath, then hurried to his side. "Did they hurt you?"

"They meant to." He grimaced. "The queen sent them to kill me."

"But if you're injured while in the mortal world..." Realization iced her bones. "The queen wanted Tam's brother to die."

"A human's death in the Realm of Faerie carries great power. She still intends to sacrifice the child, but it will be more difficult now that your friends have entered the Realm."

"Wait, what? How do you know?" Marny had to raise her voice over the sound of roaring lions, and quickly muted the vid. A little too much excitement going on without the addition of the brutal soundtrack.

Korrigan looked affronted. "I am a creature of the Realm. I am aware of what transpires there, even from my entrapment here in the human world."

"Then tell me what's happening," she said. "The beta team can't have gotten there already."

"Time moves differently in the Realm," he said. "Your mortal friends are approaching the Dark Court."

"I want you to tell me everything you can. What exactly they're doing in there, how the battle is going, all of it."

Korrigan screwed up his face and grunted. Was this the prelude to a changeling tantrum?

"Look," he said, waving at the vidscreen.

The image was blurry, and strobing light/dark/light, but Marny could make out a group of characters gathered at a crossroads. On the hill above them rose a circle of standing stones, illuminated with eerie purple light.

"Is that the beta team?" she asked, squinting to see the figures.

"Aye." Korrigan sounded a little breathless. "And see, the Faerie Rade approaches."

They looked like an army—elfin knights in shining silver armor, redcap goblins capering behind, brandishing their wickedly sharp blades. Rank after rank of faerie folk, and in the center a woman astride a tall horse, with a crown of stars blazing upon her brow.

It was like watching some epic fantasy movie—except that this was really happening, to people she cared about.

The odds didn't look good. Marny crossed her arms, trying to breathe out her anxiety. Worry wouldn't help her friends, and would only tweak her out.

The image wavered, then disappeared. She was staring at lions again, now hunting a zebra.

"Hey!" She turned to Korrigan.

"The connection is difficult to sustain," he said. "As I told you before, time is not parallel between our worlds. I am doing my best."

It was true the changeling seemed tired, his brow furrowed and his skin even paler than usual.

"Okay," Marny said. "Don't hurt yourself. But if you can get the picture back at some point, that would be great."

He nodded. "Another moment of rest, and I will try once more."

"Have a protein bar." She handed him the last one in her pocket.

Judging by how quickly he ripped the wrapper off and devoured it, channeling the Realm of Faerie was hungry work.

When he was finished, he narrowed his eyes and stared at the vidscreen.

The African plains dissolved and the Realm came back, a little distorted. Marny leaned forward, worry crashing through her. The beta-team members had been taken captive, and were tied to different standing stones at the top of the hill. They were all in a state of bad to even worse. Marny sucked in her breath at the sight of one slumped figure who looked almost dead.

"Is that Mr. Carter's character?"

"Aye."

Uncle Zeg was tied to the next stone, and Marny breathed a prayer of thanks that he was upright. He glared at the two figures standing in the center of the circle—the Dark Queen and what must certainly be the Bright King. Red and blue flames coruscated between them—

The image shivered, shifted, and now Marny saw Tam's little brother being held by the king. The fey monarch lifted a needle-sharp blade. Both Zeg and Tam rushed forward, and behind them, Jennet sliced her own radiant sword down—

A huge black dragon hovered in the sky above the standing stones. It lifted its head, its gaze piercing, and Marny swore those centuries-deep eyes looked directly at her and Korrigan. She shivered. The dragon brought its ebony wings together in a thunderclap—

The vidscreen went dark, and Korrigan crumpled to his knees.

"Korr!" Marny went to her own knees at his side, and gently lifted him.

He felt nearly hollow, all knobbles and bone in her arms.

His pale, bulging eyes blinked up at her, and he gave her a crooked smile.

"Mistress Marny, do not fear for me," he croaked.

"Is Tam's brother dying? Are you? What's happening?" She wanted to shake him for answers, but he seemed suddenly so breakable.

"The guardians between the worlds have been called," he said. "I am being pulled back to the Realm."

"Are you sure it won't kill you?" Her heart was pounding, but there was nothing she could do.

"The transition is… difficult. But I will survive."

"Does that mean the Bug is coming back to the real world?" A whoosh of relief temporarily displaced her fear, and her eyes stung with hope. With dismay.

"He will arrive here shortly," Korrigan said. "And now I must bid you farewell."

Unexpected sadness pierced her heart. "Will I ever see you again?"

Who knew that she'd become so fond of this weird, aggravating little creature? She was glad he'd managed to beat her in their last kart race. A small victory to leave the human world with.

"Our paths have tangled and twined," he said. "And the Elder has gazed into your eyes. The mark of the fey folk will be upon you now, and who knows where that might lead?"

Probably no place good.

But certainly guaranteed not to be boring.

"Take care of yourself," she said, blinking to clear her vision of tears.

"And you, mortal girl. I am happy to have called you my companion."

He grimaced, even as his body started to fade. He grew lighter and lighter in her arms, until at last she was holding only empty air.

"Goodbye, Korr," she whispered, bowing her head.

A flash of light, and something heavy landed on her, knocking her nearly off balance. She ducked a wild kick, and grabbed at the arm flailing around in front of her face. The Bug had arrived back in the real world.

"Hey, hey," she said, doing her best to channel Uncle Zeg's super-zen manner. "Calm down. It's okay—you're back."

The Bug looked up at her, eyes like Tam's in a younger, more mischievous face. He froze for a second, then bent over and started crying.

Marny hoisted him up and took him to the couch where Lara sat. Or had been sitting. She was standing now, her eyes looking more awake, her arms outstretched.

"Is that my boy?" she said, her voice strained. "Peter?"

"Mom?" The Bug lifted his wet, snotty face. "Mom!"

Before Marny could tighten her grip, he'd launched himself from her arms and tackled his mom. Luckily the plush sofa was right behind them, catching them as they went down. Tam's mom was crying too, and rubbing her son's hair.

"I'll grab some tissues," Marny said, retreating to the bathroom to give them some privacy.

She couldn't guess how aware Lara had been of Korrigan's presence. Weren't changelings glamoured so everyone believed they were the replaced child? Yet clearly Tam's mom could see the fey folk. Maybe her shutting down had more to do with an inability to believe the enchantment trying to tell her Korrigan was her own son, when he was obviously a hideous-looking fey creature.

Marny might do the same, if half her brain wanted her to believe an ugly, foul-tempered alien creature was actually her beloved kid. She'd been taken in by glamour before, and frankly, it was impressive that Lara had managed to sidestep it. Even if it had made her practically a vegetable.

"Where's Tam?" The Bug's high-pitched voice carried into the bathroom.

Marny came out with a handful of tissues and handed them to Lara. She took them, then started wiping her son's face.

"Tam should be here soon," Marny said, though she wasn't at all certain of the fact.

Sure, Korrigan had returned to the Realm and the Bug had made it home to the human world. But that didn't necessarily mean everyone on the beta team was all right. Or even alive.

She swallowed, refusing to entertain the idea for more than a second. Whatever that big dragon had been, she didn't think it would let any of her friends die.

She hoped.

"I'll get the staff to bring up some hot tea," Marny said.

"And cookies?" Tam's little brother lifted his head hopefully.

"If they have any."

For a kid who had just spent two weeks in the Dark Court, the Bug was bouncing back remarkably well.

She stepped into the hall to summon one of Spark's security guys, but paused at the sound of voices in the foyer.

"Bug?" It was Tam's voice, echoing down the hall.

Quick as a thought, Tam's little brother pushed past Marny and pelted toward the front door, footsteps slapping against the marble floor.

"Tam!" he cried.

Marny smiled as the Bug ran into Tam's arms, then smiled even wider as his mom ran forward. Lara paused in front of her boys, and placed her hand on Tam's shoulder. Without looking up, he pulled her into the embrace.

Beyond them, Marny saw Jennet watching, a look of such tenderness and joy on her face that Marny's heart stung. Tam seemed to feel Jennet's gaze on him, and lifted his head. Their gazes met, and Marny could practically see the light moving between them.

Maybe one day she would have that. She didn't know how, or when, or if Korrigan had been right that there were more fey adventures in her future.

Only way to find out was to keep moving ahead one moment, one day at a time.

Meanwhile, there was Uncle Zeg, and the bulwark of his embrace. She leaned into him and let the tight string of worry wrapping around her go.

"You won?" she asked, though she knew the answer.

"Yes." He smiled down at her, teeth white behind his fuzzy beard. "We won."

That was all anyone could ask for. It was enough to keep the world turning—and the faeries at bay for another day.

# TRINKET

## A FEYLAND TALE

Violet Yamaguchi leaned against the doorjamb of the family's computer room and tried to catch her breath. Her side ached from running all the way home from the bus stop.

The pain was worth it, though. As scheduled, the brand new FullD gaming system had been delivered. Sim chair, processor, helmet, and gloves, all hooked up and ready to go. The equipment sat gleaming in the center of the room, making their beige carpet and walls look grimy, their brown couch unspeakably worn. Even their flatscreen setup seemed like ancient tech in comparison.

The helmet reflected the room's overhead lighting in a perfect silver arc, and the gloves were studded with gemlike LEDs—rubies, sapphires, emeralds—waiting to spark into fire. Violet drew in a lungful of air scented with fresh metal and plastic.

It was the smell of promise and adventure. Of escape. Away from the drudgery of homework, away from her big brother Jay's shadow, away from the tension that chilled the house every time Mom sat down to pay bills.

Violet had scraped together her odd-jobbing money and pooled it with her brother's savings. That, plus the guilt money they'd pried out of dad (thanks to the new girlfriend), had been enough to buy the innovative FullD system. And it was beautiful.

Heart still thumping, Violet slung off her backpack and walked over to the curve of the sim chair. She ran her hand over the pristine synth-leather, smooth under her palm.

Two hours until Jay got home from soccer practice. Two hours to sink into gaming, to leave her gray-tinted life behind and explore the brand new world everyone was raving about.

She pushed her hair out of her face, her fingers brushing one of the dangly silver earrings Obaasan, her grandmother, had given her. They formed the *kanji* character for luck. Violet felt beyond lucky as she settled into the chair and powered up the system.

The gloves were comfortable, and incredibly responsive. The helmet fit perfectly, like it was custom made just for her. She pulled down the visor and gave the glove command to enter game.

### WELCOME TO FEYLAND

The words unfurled across the visor, a rich gold deepening to crimson. Flames flickered along the sides, and the letters faded to gray as though they had burned to ash. Mysterious music chimed through the speakers, and the words whirled into a flurry of leaves the color of smoke. Behind them... Violet blinked. Was that a pair of eyes, gleaming from the shadows?

The title sequence cleared to show a character-creation interface. Shaking the chill from her shoulders, she studied her options. Feyland was a fantasy-based game, and the character choices reflected that. Spellcasters and healers, warriors and rogues; standard fare. What set the game apart was the new full-simulation technology. Plus some storyline involving evil fairies, which sounded intriguing.

She scrolled past the boring-looking magic users. That was her brother's style, to stand back and inflict damage from a distance, but she preferred to get up close and messy.

The game offered four heavily-armored combat classes: Knight, Mercenary, Centurion, and Samurai. Her dad would approve of her choosing Samurai to honor her Japanese heritage—so that one was completely out. Centurions seemed too limited in their attack styles, and Mercenaries didn't use shields. Which left her the Knight.

A sense of rightness warmed her belly as she read.

*KNIGHT: Skilled at feats of arms, noble, courageous, and true, the Knight can best almost any enemy in battle. Only magic can bring this hero to their knees - but even then, the Knight's sword may prove of greater power.*

Below the description stood a basic character, ready to be modified to her specifications. She played with the options, adding detail to the avatar. Her Knight would be female, of course, tall and strong. But not too built—quickness could usually beat strength, if there was room to move. Long dark hair, braided back, and the eyes she'd always wanted—a piercing, icy blue. With a flick of her finger, she put the final touches on her new self.

The character bounced slightly up and down, and Violet smiled. Now for a name—nothing too girly. She liked using variations of her own name when she gamed.

She double-clicked her thumb and index finger, the universal glove command to bring up the keyboard. V-I-

E, she typed. Vie. Good enough. She closed the interface and studied her avatar. Yes, her Knight looked good, all tough and decked out in shiny silver armor. A sword hung at her side, and she had a grim-looking shield strapped to her back, plus a quiver of arrows and a long, sleek bow.

*Character complete. Enter game?*

She pulled in a breath, then tipped her thumb up. *Yes.*

A fanfare of trumpets blared as her vision went golden. The pit of her stomach roiled with an odd, queasy sensation. Maybe she should have grabbed a glass of water when she got home, instead of dashing right to the computer room.

Then all discomfort was forgotten as her character arrived in Feyland.

She stood in a clearing surrounded by white-barked trees. The sky was bright blue overhead, the grass a vivid green. Wind moved across the trees, the leaves riffling silver. A bird swooped past, singing, and she could almost feel the warm air against her face.

Violet turned in a slow circle, taking it all in. There was nothing like seeing a new world for the first time. The emerald grass beneath her feet was starred with blue flowers, and she was encircled by bright red mushrooms dotted with white; a faerie ring. On the far side of the clearing, a fern-lined pathway led between the pillar-like trunks of the pale trees. Shafts of sunlight slanted through, giving the forest a dreamy, peaceful look.

This was the best simulation she'd ever experienced, no question.

But she'd played enough games to know that appearances were deceiving—especially beautifully quiet scenes. Before she headed out, she needed to figure out how to use her sword.

Hard on the heels of that thought, her character drew the blade and settled into a combat stance, shield strapped to her right arm. Violet blinked in surprise. Not only had that been effortless, the game had picked up her physical cues and put the sword in her dominant left hand.

Impressive.

She made a few experimental swipes, the blade swishing through the air. It was scary how easily she controlled her character. The boundary between herself and her avatar felt gossamer thin. She *was* the Knight, ready to embark on a journey through an enchanted landscape.

Grinning, Violet sheathed her sword. So far, Feyland was everything she'd hoped. She jumped over the mushroom boundary and headed down the path. Soft moss cushioned her footsteps, and the quiet between the trees was broken by the liquid trilling of some unseen bird.

And a high, muffled laugh.

She spun around, hand on the pommel of her sword. "Who's there?"

No answer—but the branches above her head rustled, and she glimpsed a ball of shimmering light. She glanced up, then dodged to the side as a dozen acorns dropped. Most of them missed, but one or two pinged against her armor.

More laughter, and not just one voice—the mirth was in chiming harmony. Violet stepped back, and this time saw several balls of silver light hovering among the branches. She squinted. Inside each ball, surrounded by the shimmery glow, was a tiny, winged figure.

They didn't seem dangerous, unless they landed an acorn

in her eye. Keeping a wary watch overhead, Violet continued along the path. No more nut missiles dropped from the foliage, but she could hear the high-pitched laughter above her in the rustling branches as she strode through the woods.

The pale trunks began thinning out, showing glimpses of rolling green hills beyond. When the forest ended, she stepped out of the trees to find a cottage right in front of her, complete with thatched roof and diamond-paned windows. Very fairytale.

A small, goblin-like creature squatted on the doorstep. It had skin like old leather, long ears, and a nose that curved sharply downward, almost meeting an equally pointed chin. It watched her approach with dark, unblinking eyes, but didn't seem about to attack.

If this was like other fantasy games she'd played, the creature would give her a quest to complete, or direct her which way to go. The fact that there was nothing hovering over the goblin's head made it hard to tell what to do; no icon telling her what the creature's function was, or if it were friend or foe. On the other hand, the lack of big graphic cues sure contributed to the immersive experience.

One hand resting lightly on her sword, she stopped a few feet from the steps.

"Hello," she said to the creature.

It blinked once, then spoke in a high, creaky voice. "Greetings, adventurer, and welcome to the Realm. I am the goblin called Hob."

"I'm—"

"Vie the Brave," the goblin interrupted. "When you set foot in this world, your presence was noted."

There was an uncanny ring to his words she didn't like.

On the up side, though, it looked like she'd already gained an in-game title. Vie the Brave. She liked the sound of it.

"Do you seek a quest?" Hob asked.

"I do."

The goblin smiled, showing sharply-pointed teeth. "Heed what I now say. Follow the path beyond yonder hill, to a field of trefoil herbs. One among them has four leaves. Pluck that one only, and no other. Understood?"

"Yes."

She shifted, a chill shadow touching her as a cloud passed in front of the sun. It was crazy how much sensory stimulation this game provided. No wonder people were calling Feyland the best game of the century.

"Go now, and return to me with the herb," Hob said, a gleam in his dark eyes. "And 'ware the Pixies."

Violet turned away from the cottage and continued on the path. She glanced over her shoulder once, to see Hob still sitting on the front step, knobby knees crossed, his dark eyes fixed on her. She was glad when the path curved between two hillocks, removing her from the goblin's sight. Creepy little creature, and hard to tell if he was good or bad.

One thing she knew. Her quest might *seem* easy, but it would be dangerous—she hadn't needed Hob to tell her to beware. The game wouldn't have given her weapons if she wasn't going to need them.

The path descended into a small valley carpeted with clover, and Violet laughed softly. Trefoil herbs—clover. And she was supposed to find a four-leafed one. Classic. A few fat bees buzzed around the pinkish- white flowers, but that was fine—bugs didn't bother her. On the far side of the meadow a bit of sky was reflected in a tiny round lake, a single blue eye staring straight up.

She'd start with the left hand side of the path and work her way around toward the water. Despite the peacefulness of the scene, she kept her senses alert as she scanned the plants. A sweet, faint scent drifted up from the flowers; warm and slightly dusty. Her shadow was sharp against the clover, etched there by the sun hanging motionless in the clear blue dome of sky.

The peace quickly turned to drudgery, leaves and stems and flowers blurring together. Her hands were tired of riffling through the clover, but she was almost to the mini-lake; a good point to stop and rest.

The water was absolutely transparent. Violet bent over the surface, making sure no clovers grew on the bottom. Her avatar's face stared at her, black hair, dark eyes.... Wait a second. Hadn't she chosen blue?

She frowned, and her reflection frowned back. Either the character creation was glitchy, or she'd hit the wrong button by mistake. Oh well—she'd make another avatar at some point, with the right eyes.

A light breeze ruffled the grasses, and she stifled a sigh. This was the most tedious quest ever. She hated the ones in other games where she had to kill hundreds of creatures just to win one item, but crawling through a meadow of identical plants, no matter how idyllic, was worse.

Only one way to get it done, though. Violet shook out her hands and started searching again. She'd only gone a little farther when she spotted a four-leafed clover. *Finally!* She picked it and held it up—only to see that one of the leaves was slightly separated. Not a four-leafer after all. The game had tricked her.

The earth trembled. She dropped the clover and hastily got to her feet, drawing her sword. She was about to discover the consequences of picking the wrong plant. The ground in front of her seethed, the foliage melting away to reveal bare earth that bulged menacingly outward, like a bubble about to pop.

It exploded with a *whump*, spraying dirt everywhere. A pebble bounced off her cheek, and she hurriedly stepped back —then lifted her blade as two hideous creatures clambered from the newly-formed hole. They were squat and ferocious, wearing rough leather armor and carrying long pikes. The one in front grinned, sharp-toothed and evil-eyed, and lifted his weapon.

Now she *really* wished she hadn't picked the wrong clover.

No point in waiting for the attack. She rushed forward, shouting her *kiai*. Maybe it was the force of her swing, or that the creatures in Feyland were programmed to recognize Karate yells, but her target fell back. Unfortunately for him, he teetered on the edge of the hole.

"Grahr!" he cried as he tumbled backward, out of sight.

She grinned. One down, one to go.

The remaining creature narrowed his eyes and circled away from the hole. Violet leaned forward, putting her weight on the balls of her feet, and raised her shield. Just in time. Her enemy charged, faster than she'd anticipated. She blocked his pike thrust and the barbed head grated across her shield. Her angle wasn't quite right, and the barbs grazed her forearm, in the gap above her gauntlets. A bright zing of pain went through her—not enough to distract her from the fight, but enough to let her know she'd been injured. Feyland had an incredible neural interface.

She rushed her opponent in a quick counterattack. The trick was to stay in close and on the offensive. The creature yelped as her sword connected, nicking his arm. Green blood oozed from the cut, but it wasn't severe enough to take her enemy out. He lashed out again, and Violet whirled into a roundhouse kick—surprisingly easy, even wearing armor. Her heel smashed into his elbow, and he dropped his pike.

"Ha," Violet said, brandishing her sword.

The creature's eyes widened—no wicked grin on his face now. He whirled and jumped into the hole, abandoning his weapon.

The earth shut, like a mouth smacking closed, sending up a spray of dust. When the air cleared, there was no sign of the attack. The meadow lay quiet around her, the clover undisturbed. Even the pike was gone.

Okay then. Time to find her clover—a real four-leafer this time.

She almost plucked two more fake ones before finally discovering a clover that looked like the real thing. Violet lay on her belly and put her face right up to the plant, the flowers tickling her nose, and counted the leaves. One, two, three. Four.

She stood up before she picked it, so she'd be ready if anything came at her again.

Her fingers snapped the stem, and she straightened, holding her breath. The air shimmered faintly. She moved the clover to her right hand so her sword arm would be free, though it wouldn't be easy to fight if she had to hold onto the plant.

Immediately, the clover disappeared. Her heart bumped up —she couldn't lose her quest item now!

In the lower left corner of her interface, a letter *I* appeared, blinking. *I* for inventory? She selected it and a series of empty boxes materialized. Empty except one, which held the four-leafed clover. She let out a relieved breath. Just by thinking about it, she'd been able to store the clover away.

She inspected the other boxes, then closed her inventory. The designers of Feyland didn't believe in over-gearing a player. No food, no drink, no extra potions or talismans to help her fight. This was a weird game—super stripped-down in some ways, and yet so immersive she felt as though she was *there*, wandering around an enchanted land. Seriously, she could even sense the soft touch of the wind against her cheek.

Birds trilled overhead—except that birds didn't sound high and chiming. Violet looked up. Seven shimmering balls of light flew toward her; the glowing faerie-creatures she had seen earlier. Were these the Pixies that Hob had warned her about?

The balls of light came at her, closer and closer, without slowing. She took a step back.

"Hello?" she said. "Um—can I help you?"

One of the Pixies dived right at her face. Violet ducked.

"Hey! No need for that."

The only response was a giggle. Another ball of light descended to give her hair a sharp tug, while a third buzzed around her armor, no doubt looking for a chink.

"Cut it out." Violet batted at the annoying creatures, but the Pixies danced and darted away.

Fine, then. She drew her sword and waved it.

"I'm not afraid to use this," she warned.

Instead of deterring the Pixies, the sight of her sword seemed to inflame them. Two of them tangled painfully in her hair, four kept whizzing around her, and the last one tried to creep into the gap above her gauntlet.

She shook the creature off, then swiped at the others with her blade. It was like trying to swat flies with an open umbrella. The glowing Pixies zipped away faster than her eye could follow, then moved right back in to pester her. Even her shield was too cumbersome, and provided no barrier to the aggravating motes of light.

Violet glanced up the pathway. Hob's cottage wasn't too far—just over the hill and around the corner. Worth making a run for, since using her sword against the tiny glowing faeries was useless.

"Look over there!" she called, pointing across the clover-strewn meadow.

It actually worked. The Pixies stopped dive-bombing her, and two of them headed away to investigate. Violet turned and pelted along the path.

High, angry screeches followed her. It didn't take long for her tiny tormentors to catch up, but she bent low and kept going, her sword bouncing at her side. She crested the hill, trying not to pant. At least her armor felt like regular clothing rather than weighty pieces of metal.

The Pixies started going for her face, whizzing past and pinching her cheeks, tweaking her nose. She put her arm up to shield herself, but she couldn't run without seeing where she was going.

One Pixie hovered by her ear, humming like a musical mosquito.

"Ow!" Sharp pain tore through her earlobe.

Violet clapped her hand to her ear, gritted her teeth, and kept going. Maybe she should have made a magic-using character after all, because the skills of a Knight sure weren't designed to combat Pixies. A big magical fireball, now that would work. Fry the creatures out of the air. She didn't care how cute they were—they had gone past the point of forgiveness.

Ahead, Hob's cottage came into view; the white plaster shining in the sun, the multi-paned windows sparkling. The goblin still sat on the doorstep, his black eyes unreadable. He rose, lifted a long-fingered hand, and spoke in a guttural language. The Pixies squeaked and fled toward the pale-trunked forest, seven lights shimmering into the deeper shadows of the woods until they were gone.

Violet rubbed her throbbing ear, glad to see the last of them. She trudged the remaining few yards and stopped in front of Hob.

"Greetings, Vie the Brave," the goblin said in his creaky-hinged voice. "Have you accomplished the task I set you?"

"I have."

Violet toggled open her inventory and handed Hob the four-leaf clover. He inspected the plant, turning it side-to-side, then looked up and smiled at her; a hideous expression on his ugly face.

"Your quest is complete, adventurer. You have won access to the second level of Feyland. I shall transport you there." He lifted his hands, his fingers inscribing glowing runes in the air.

"Wait," she said. "Can't you tell me about—"

A thick golden haze surrounded her, blocking out Hob and his cottage, the woods, even the sun-bedazzled sky. So much for her questions about the game. She wasn't sure she liked Feyland's learn-as-you-go approach.

The light flared, then faded away to reveal a deep, piney forest. The air was rich with the scent of cedar and sap. Sunlight sifted through the branches, scattering dappled coins of light on the forest floor. She stood in the center of another ring of white-speckled red mushrooms—apparently the portal to the next level of the game.

She wanted to jump out of the faerie ring and follow the mossy path edged with purple flowers, but the smart part of her knew she'd better log off. Jay would be home soon, insisting on his turn. He'd rudely kick her off the sim equipment whether she was at a good stopping point or not. She'd lost way too much progress on various games to take the chance.

The beckoning path, and the next adventure, would have to wait.

With a silent sigh, Violet slid her fingers together in the command to exit game. Instead of simply returning her to the starting screen, a dizzying vortex of light whirled around her. If that was the game designers' idea of a cool trick, she'd prefer to pass.

Finally, her vision cleared to show the depressingly ordinary walls of the computer room. She sat forward and stripped off the gaming gloves, then lifted the helmet and set it on its stand. Her right arm stung, and she glanced down to see an angry red scratch marring her skin. Weird. Somehow the glove must have scraped her. She inspected it, pulling it on and off, but couldn't detect anything sharp. Maybe a wire had accidentally poked her, then gotten re-seated.

Her ear hurt too, and she rubbed it. Wait—where was her

earring? Had the helmet yanked it out while she was playing? That would explain the sharp pain when the Pixies had been tormenting her.

Violet picked up the helmet and shook it, then turned it over and inspected the lining. She slid the visor up and down, felt the lining by the speakers. Nothing.

She couldn't have lost one of her earrings—they were her favorite pair!

Disappointment clogging her throat, she knelt on the carpet and searched all around the FullD system. No luck.

The front door slammed open, and she heard Jay calling goodbye to his friends. Violet rose. She must have lost her earring earlier, maybe when she slung her backpack off. It would turn up.

Or maybe she'd lost it in-game.

The fanciful notion made her shake her head. *Silly.* No matter how immersive it seemed, Feyland was only a simulation.

SEVEN PIXIES FLITTED through the branches of the pale-trunked trees. They spoke in high-pitched chiming, a language of mirth and mischief. Something sparkled in the air, tossed back and forth between the glowing faeries; something long and silver, hooked at one end. Something precious.

A trinket, stolen from the human world.

The End

# BREA'S TALE: ARRIVAL

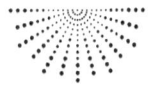

## A FEYLAND TALE

THE FAERIE GIRL arrived in a bubble of cold blue light, a barrier between herself and the dangers of the mortal world. Before she could take a breath, the magic dissipated, revealing crumbling structures and pitted pavement beneath a dimly-lit sky. She shivered as the clammy air pressed against her skin. It seemed to be night, though there was no moon to guide her, no pinpricks of stars shining steady overhead.

The air smelled wrong, tainted with rot and strange metallic fumes. The light was peculiar too, an orange wash smeared across the clouds. But the sounds were the most foreign things: monstrous growls approaching and receding, mortal voices raised in shouts of fear or anger, the rushing pulse of something too mechanical to be waves pushing against the shore.

In one hand she clutched a silver medallion inset with a moonstone, the chain trickling through her fingers. More than a talisman, it was a means to return back to the enchanted world from which she had come. Precious beyond words.

Blinking, she tried to recall her name. Her human name, which once she had worn as easily as a woolen shawl wrapped about her shoulders. Once—before she had slipped into the Realm of Faerie and lost all need for human things.

Brea had been her name. Brea Cairgead.

She stood unsteadily on her two human legs and tried to quell the nervousness prickling through her. The wrongness of this world made her heart beat fast, her gossamer garment no protection from the night. Every instinct shouted at her to flee, to flick her tail and dart to the concealing coolness of the deep shadows.

Yet even if there had been a sheltering pool nearby, she was trapped in this mortal form. There would be no tail, no fins, no undulating through the bright waters. Not until she completed her quest and was allowed to return home to the Realm of Faerie.

Ah, but she was so weak compared to most members of the Dark Court. Their mocking words still echoed in her thoughts.

"That one?" The black-mouthed banshee had shrieked with glee. "She'll not last a day in the human world!"

"Aye, she'll be eaten in a trice." One of the redcap goblins licked his lips, then bared his needle-sharp teeth. "Maybe I'll follow her in and do the job."

"No need," a fungal-covered hooligan sneered. "She'll return defeated by the next moon, mark my words. Then the queen might give her to you as a plaything."

The Dark Queen's cold voice cut through the babble. "This maid betrayed the Realm, and must pay the price. Whether she succeeds or not, I lay this geas upon her. Should she fail, she shall be banished to walk the Shadowlands forever."

The court tittered at the queen's words. Their bright, avid gazes had fixed on Brea, anticipating her disgraceful return, ready to revel in the crushing bitterness of her failure.

She must not fail.

Though she might have been mortal once, was she not now a creature of the Realm? She had a few small magics to call upon, paltry though they might be. Lifting her face to the absent moon, she prayed they would be enough.

She was alone and afraid, but she would not let this strange new place defeat her. She pulled in a breath of tainted air, trying not to cough at the sour taste. First, she must find a safe haven. Once hidden, she could begin to explore this city of the humans, fortify herself, and discover a way to fulfill the queen's commands.

Something moved in the shadowed mouth of a nearby alleyway.

"Well, well. What's a pretty thing like you doing out here in the Exe?" The voice was smooth and full of menace.

Brea whirled, breath clogging in her throat, to see a pock-faced man leaning against the crumbling wall. His smile and the blade of his knife glinted in the dim light. From down the alley came the clack of rubble dislodged and soft footsteps. Two more men emerged, young and feral-looking.

Any brief notion that she might be able to use these humans fled. She was prey here, not predator.

"Only wearing a nightie, too." The first man's smile widened. "Sleepwalking, love? We can show you back to bed."

The others laughed, something brutish in the sound.

"What's in her hand?" one of them asked.

The first man straightened and began to approach. "Are you a runaway, been stealing jewelry? Let's have a look."

No. She could not lose the medallion.

Brea gulped air, then turned and ran. Blindly, stupidly, stumbling over discarded metal pipes that burned her bare feet. Behind her came the sounds of pursuit, the men tossing banter back and forth. There was no doubt they would catch her.

Moon and stars, please let her find a safe place!

A noisesome puddle slicked her feet with oil, and she scraped her arm upon a coil of sharp wire. Tears leaked from the corners of her eyes.

Heart hammering, she veered around a corner, then let out a cry of relief. A tree stood in an abandoned square ahead, branches reaching into the eerie orange sky. She forced herself to run faster, and heard her pursuers accelerate in response. Closer, closer...

Gasping, she fetched up at the tree, her hands going to the rough bark for reassurance. For power.

She cried out again, but not in relief. The tree was dead, a husk with withered roots reaching into the poisoned soil. There was no living energy she could pull forth to help her defeat her enemies. Only soot and dust.

The men rushed up and surrounded her, the leader coming to stand before her.

"Enough," he said. His breath came easy in his chest, and Brea bitterly rued her new human form, that could scarcely run a handful of minutes without tiring.

He caught her wrist, and she yelped at the touch of metal against her skin. Bright spots of pain drilled into her body from where his iron-ringed hand clasped her arm, and she yanked herself free, medallion still gripped tightly in her closed fist.

Brea closed her eyes briefly, old fear washing through her. She had been chased by brigands one fateful day, long ago. Caught then, too. But this time there was no silent, sacred water waiting to welcome her in. No liquid transformation that could be wrought.

"Take her back to the rest of the pack?" one of the younger men asked.

"Head Jackal will want to see what we caught," the first man said. "Too bad she don't have a wrist chip. Looks more valuable than she is. Though whatever she's got…"

He grabbed her again, and pried her fingers open. The silver medallion was revealed upon her palm, gleaming in the faint light. The runes inscribed on the surface were barely visible, but the moonstone shone as if lit from within.

Despair washed through her, but she pushed it away. She *must* escape. She had no choice.

And she was no longer a frightened mortal girl, unaware of her own magic. She was a creature of Faerie now, one of the fey folk.

Unfortunately, the medallion she held was no use, despite the powerful spell it contained. The talisman's magic could not be turned to any purpose but the one it was made for—to send her back to the Dark Court. Should she return now, her fate would be sealed. Goblin's plaything, then eternal banishment to a land of dust and shadows.

"Pretty." The man reached to pluck it from her hand.

Heart pounding in her chest, Brea closed her fingers around the medallion. Fiercely, she summoned the power of the invisible stars, the small, rugged weeds pushing up through cracks in the concrete, the salty rush of blood under the men's skin.

*Glimmer and fade, come to my aid. Mortal flesh turn to air, bear me safely from here.*

She half closed her eyes and willed herself to become a wisp of shadow, a tatter of moonlight. The dead tree pulsed and shivered, the weeds on the sidewalk wilted over, spent. A violent shiver wracked her body, and then she disappeared, her form now invisible, yet still present.

A breath of wind curled around the dead tree, and she caught the tail of it and let it pull her out of reach.

"Where'd she go?" the first man yelled.

"You were supposed to be holding her," one of the youths said.

"She was right here, dammit. Don't just stand there, find her."

They split up, searching the shadows, their footsteps angry over the ground. They would not catch her. Already she was slipping beyond their reach, carried away on the breeze.

"Take me to a safe haven," she whispered, fighting her body's urge to become solid once more.

Not yet. She must find a hiding place.

The wind eddied and turned, bearing her first high, then low. Lights of human habitation spread like a blanket, but the place she was traveling over was dark. That would serve well enough—for was she not a creature who dwelt on the edge of the Dark Realm? Here in the mortal world, darkness would be her ally.

At last the breeze slid through the broken-out window of an abandoned building. Thrice around it went, like an animal making its den, then whispered away to nothing.

Unable to maintain her ethereal state, Brea tumbled to the cold cement floor and landed painfully on her hands and knees. She shuddered, breathing fast to combat the sudden sickness in her belly. Curses upon this ungainly human body she now wore, bound by gravity and bone.

Finally the feeling passed and she sat up, alert for any sign of danger.

The growls and rumbles of mortal machines were distant here, muted to a dull ache. She sensed no trace of the men who'd tried to ensnare her. Other humans dwelt near to her hiding place—she could feel the sickly yellow pulse of their presence—but they were wounded and worn, presenting no immediate threat.

Exhaustion crashed down on her like the flume of a waterfall. The medallion slipped gently from her hand and clinked upon the cement.

She was safe—for now.

THIRST BURNED THROUGH HER, waking her from confused dreams of the Dark Queen's midnight gaze, Puck's impish smile.

But she was no longer in the Realm, as her aching mortal body proved.

*Water.*

The need pushed her to her feet, and she stood a moment, surveying her hiding place. The silver medallion lay gleaming against the cracked, stained floor. She picked it up, magicked a pocket into her gossamer garment, and tucked the talisman away.

Wan yellow light crept in through the broken doorway, spilled over the jutting overhang of the ruined roof. The sky overhead was blue, and she caught her breath. For so long she had lived in the sweet dimness of the Dusk Vale, she'd nearly forgotten the color of the daytime sky.

The sight gave her the strength to step over the rubbled threshold. Outside, another dead tree rose beside the wall of her shelter, its dry, dead leaves whispering together in the faint breeze. The air smelled of decay and things long abandoned.

She turned in a slow circle, examining the half-ruined building, the withered tree, the broken walkway where thin grasses struggled up between the cracks.

Yes. This place would serve as her temporary home.

There was much to do in order to make it a place of some comfort, but first she must find water.

The oil-slimed puddles she sensed in a nearby alleyway made her wrinkle her nose in disgust. No, she could not stomach such tainted liquid. She closed her eyes and hummed softly. *Cool water, pure water, whither might you be?*

The shimmer of an answer came from deeper inside her shelter, though it was masked with the forbidding hum of iron. Brea followed the song into a small room where tiny insects scuttled. A white trough lay within, and a smaller basin. The scent of water rose strongly from the walls.

How to reach it?

She folded her arms and studied the basin, reluctantly coming to the conclusion that the metal handles protruding from the wall would release the water. Yet she could not touch them without burning herself.

"Think, girl," she said, the sound of her own voice soft in the dimness.

Back in the main room, she cast about for an answer. The

tiny red heartbeats of small rodents pulled her to the far corner, where mice nested in a pile of torn rags.

"I am sorry," she said to them, "but I'm in need of your bedding. Perhaps you ought to find another dwelling place."

She did not particularly relish the thought of sharing her new quarters with the mice, anyway. Using a bit of magic, she nudged them forth, a half-dozen furry, squeaking bodies that made for the door without much protest.

Gingerly picking up the rags, Brea carried them to the doorway and shook them vigorously. Despite her weakness, she laid a quick cleansing enchantment upon the dingy bits of cloth. The effort left her shaking, and she leaned against the doorjamb for a long moment, letting the pale sun warm her skin.

*Water.*

Yes, yes. Somewhat unsteadily she went back into the small room. Gritting her teeth at the painful proximity of cold iron, she wrapped the rags about one handle, and turned. It squeaked with disuse, and a coughing rattle came from within the walls.

A trickle emerged, stained with minerals, and Brea turned the handle harder. *Please.*

Glorious fresh water spilled forth into the basin.

She turned her face to the sky, to the invisible stars, and breathed a prayer of thanks. Then, careful to avoid the spigot, she stuck her hands into that life-giving stream and gulped greedily from her cupped palms. Peace and strength flowed into her. Smiling, she leaned forward and let the water run over her head, down into her eyes and grateful mouth.

At last, replete, she shut the water off and shook her wet hair away from her face. Now she could start exploring her surroundings and make a plan of action. For the first time, a flutter of excitement went through her.

It had been a long, long time since she'd inhabited the human world. And although she was a fey creature now, there was, perhaps, a kernel of loneliness in her heart. An ache belonging to the mortal part of herself, whether she wanted it or not.

But yearnings aside, she needed to ward her shelter for safety and protection. With renewed magic coursing through her, she hummed and wove her spells. First, a layer of aversions strung like spider silk around the perimeter, so that any human wandering by would have no interest in exploring further, and would turn away.

Then more protections about the threshold and broken windows, and where the roof gaped open, keeping away anything that would mean her harm.

It was not the kind of magic that would leap and attack, like a guard dog, but a deflection—a pebble placed in the current, that the water might run around without causing any harm.

Once her wards were complete she could no longer ignore the fact that she must now venture into the human world. She would need a disguise, of course, a glamour to pull across her features. Judging by the events of last night, it would need to be something fierce and forbidding.

After a moment's pondering, she combined the worst features of her three pursuers into one hulking, ugly human male, and let the guise settled over her shoulders.

Then, ignoring the tremor in her belly, she stepped out into the light.

As she had thought, the area around her shelter was

mostly deserted. She turned toward the hum, the heartbeat of the city, and began to walk.

Two blocks down the empty street she passed a building filled with the sluggish dreams of yellow-eyed men. Their thoughts put her in mind of a nest of chilled wasps; slow to rouse, but once angered, difficult to escape. She resolved to give them a wide berth.

Further on, a hollow-cheeked woman rummaged through a pile of trash on the street. She shrank back as Brea strode past, fear rising off her in sour waves.

The sounds of human machines grew louder. Brea hesitated at the edge of an area pulsing with angry red light, invisible to the mortal gaze. This was the province of the men who had wanted to capture her, their territory marked by sigils painted on the nearby buildings—angular and bright, and full of warning.

She stood a moment, then turned aside. Even in her forbidding human guise, she would not be able to pass safely through.

Sooner than she was ready for, she went from the crumbling neighborhood into more normal human habitation. First, a few scrawny children who darted into sagging houses at her approach, then men gathered about hulks of painful iron in the street, then women moving hurriedly, bags of provisions beneath their arms.

Ahead the rush and roar grew louder, as did the vibrations of cold iron grating against her bones. When she came to the source, she stopped dead in surprise.

Horseless wagons made of metal charged up and down the streets, growling and emitting noxious fumes. Humans rode inside, hurtling at abnormal speeds. Brea's belly clenched at the thought of being enclosed in so much iron.

The tang of it in the air smote her, and she swayed, dizziness shading her vision. Her mind darted this way and that, a minnow trapped in a puddle. She was defenseless, prey for any passing hunger.

Breathing shallowly through her mouth, she whirled and ran back the way she had come. Past the women and men, past the startled children, until enough crumbling brick and concrete was between her and the inimical hum of the metal.

Panting, she stopped beside a brightly painted wall and bent, hands on her knees. This would never do. How could she perform her task and obey the queen's bidding when she was overcome the moment she stepped into the heart of the human city? Already she could hear the mocking titters of the Dark Court denizens.

*Think, girl*, she told herself. Despite the general disbelief in her abilities, surely the Dark Queen would not have sent her on an entirely fruitless endeavor.

Which meant that, somehow, she had the strength to succeed.

Mortals did not feel the effect of cold iron. Once, she'd been one of them. She did not think she could ever be completely human, not after she had discovered her own magic and dwelt so long in the Realm; centuries, judging by the world she now found herself in.

But perhaps she might be able to become *more* human.

Not here, though, in an alleyway where she could still hear the roar of the metal contraptions. Shoulders slumped, she picked her way back into the Exe and the bare welcome of the shelter she had claimed as her own.

I<small>T</small> <small>TOOK</small> three days and three nights for her to find the balance.

The first day, she opened the hole in her heart, the one filled with human sorrow and loss, and dived in.

Her skin tightened and burned, her vision narrowed, the colors fading, and she could no longer feel the slow, steady pulse of the earth and stars. She stared at her blunt, human hands, smelled the stink of mortal fear, and panicked revulsion rose in her throat, nearly choking her.

*No.* Too much of herself was imbued with magic. Without it, she became nothing but a feeble human girl. As such, it would be impossible to carry out the queen's bidding. With great relief, she backed away from the edge of mortality. Cool silver closed over her, like the waters of a still pool, and she collapsed, exhausted, upon the hard floor.

She woke, aching, with the light of a new dawn. The concrete was cold beneath her, and the need for water burned her throat. Wincing, she rose and went to the bathing room. Clearly she'd gone too far into her own humanity the day before.

The water ran clear, and she caught some in a broken cup she had found the previous day on her way home. As she drank, careful of the jagged porcelain edge, she pondered.

What if she embraced her heritage, the shapechanging magic borne in her blood?

If this attempt went awry as the last one had, she should ensure there was sufficient water at hand. It would be the utmost stupidity to die flopping about the floor, suffocating from the harsh air.

She cobbled together a rough plug for the bathing trough, then filled it halfway with water. Perched on the side, she began to hum a liquid lullaby. Although she'd never met her mother, the woman had gifted her with the power to transform. Her mother's heritage was tied to the sea, but Brea had been unable to activate her own ability within the salty brine.

Instead, the pure water of the sacred spring had seen her first transformation. That location, and her half-human blood, might explain why she was not a mer-creature—nor a nixie, a water hag, or a nymph. Instead she was a girl who might become a flashing silver fish from one heartbeat to the next.

With that thought, she changed, slipping down into the water. There were no sheltering shadows, no waving tendrils of plants, no swirling currents to soothe her scales. Only plain water, carrying an unpleasant tang to her piscean senses, though it was safe enough for her to drink.

A sigh became bubbles, and then she sat in the water, human once more. Her gossamer dress clung wetly to her legs, and her hair dripped down her back.

Transforming to her fish form was no answer, either, though she felt much refreshed. Still, a silver trout could not do as the queen commanded.

Neither could an aching and non-magical human body.

Frowning, Brea rose from the tub. Despite her makeshift stopper, the water was slowly slipping down the drain. She tugged the plug out, then went to the main room of her shelter, leaving a trail of droplets in her wake.

If she were to embrace a greater degree of mortality, she would need more than a hard floor in an empty room. Such austerity was all very well for creatures of shadow and starlight, or fish who could swim away and find a home in any watery embrace. But for the magical mortal she must become, some comfort was in order.

She settled cross-legged on the stained cement, calling up memories of when she was human.

A bed was a necessity, and not just a thin straw mattress covered with a scratchy woolen blanket that still smelled of sheep. She would need clothing, and something to store it in. Someplace safe to keep the medallion—a small chest, perhaps —that she might bespell with protections. A drinking vessel that did not threaten to cut her mouth with each sip. Those would make a fine start.

*And how will you insinuate yourself into the human world and begin the queen's quest?* She banished the voice, though it caused a flutter of fear in her chest. First things first.

Now, while the strength of her magic flowed through her, she should attempt going among mortals again. But not on foot, and not into the area she had tried before.

*She hummed again, and let herself become light as a wisp, a glimmer. Breeze, bear me forth, high and safe overhead, to find what I seek, garments bright—and a bed.*

Clumsy, perhaps, but adequate. No one at the Dark Court had accused her of elegance in her spellcasting.

The obliging wind floated her up and out of the gap in her crumbling roof. From a height, the blight spreading over the Exe was plain. Decay, neglect, and loneliness—the ideal place to hide. She floated south, then east, trusting the air to carry her. Indeed, it was a much better solution than donning a glamour and trying to navigate the human world on foot. A pity she could not set her magical mark upon the mortals as she drifted past, but this form had its limitations.

She realized her mistake as she hovered before a window made of glass so smooth it was nearly invisible. Displayed inside were various items of clothing, some of them so garishly colored they assaulted her senses.

As a wisp of wind, she could not touch anything. Which meant she could not carry away garments, or bedding, or any of her purchases whatsoever.

But at least she could find the location of the vendors of such things. Perhaps even more importantly, she might observe the humans going about their business. The metal vehicles did not weaken her as much as they had the day before. She was growing stronger, and her ephemeral form seemed to buffer her from the worst effects.

A woman wearing a green coat passed beneath her. Brea caught the fragrance of lemon and spices in her hair, and decided to follow.

As luck would have it, the woman entered one of the shops lining the street. Brea managed to drift inside before the strange glass doors whooshed shut. Then she paused, glad she had no lungs, for she would have gasped aloud.

Row upon row of skirts and trousers, dresses and scarves; more than a hundred people could wear in a lifetime. Beyond the ranks of clothing stood cases overflowing with jewelry, colorful gems glinting amid the sheen of precious metals. And beyond even that, like some palace filled with wonders, dozens of beds, each one made up more opulently than the last.

The sheer abundance was dizzying. Chieftains of old would have fallen weeping to their knees, or gone to war a thousand times over for a fraction of the wealth on display.

"Look, mama." A young child holding her mother's hand, pointed to where Brea hovered near bank of lights. "Sparkly!"

"Yes, dear." The distracted parent didn't bother glancing up.

Even if she had, would she have seen Brea's shimmer? Unwilling to risk the chance, she wafted away toward the beds. She passed a corner filled with goblets and ornate plates, and an area where intricately patterned rugs spilled carelessly across the floor.

A constant ringing noise pulled her to an intersection in the center of the vast store. From her vantage point overhead, she watched as busy shop girls imprisoned behind a counter placed the various customers' goods into bags.

She drifted closer, trying to determine the system of payment. Certainly there was no barter here, no exchanging a bag of onions for a length of woven cloth, or a salted fish for an apple.

Instead, some of the buyers waved their hands in some kind of magical alchemy she could not discern. Others, however, tendered slim silvery cards that seemed to serve as currency. Puzzlingly, the shopkeeper girls always handed the cards back at the end of the transaction.

Descending, Brea tried to catch a clearer view of the card.

"Brr." One of the shop girls pulled her sweater more tightly about her shoulders. "Can you believe management has the air on at this time of year?"

"I don't feel anything," her nearest companion said.

Realizing her presence was being sensed, Brea veered away, rising once more to the bright rows of lights.

A flicker of light and sound beckoned her attention to the

far wall where a row of framed images were displayed. Yet these were not motionless portraits, but living depictions, seeming so real she might drift into the very picture and be transported to a different place. What strange human magic was this?

One screen showed an earnest young man leaping through the trees, pursued by fierce wild creatures. Another showed a beautiful woman declaring her love for a bored-looking fellow dressed all in black, while a third featured a disembodied voice describing a scene full of rubble and smoke.

A bright flicker of color made her turn and watch, bemused, as a chipper girl extolled the virtues of a cream one could apply to hands and face. That seemed to end quickly, and another woman appeared, holding up a glass of green liquid called SupaVitaWata, and drinking deeply. Then a boy floating above the ground on something termed a *g-board*.

It was overwhelming, yet she could not tear herself away. Information washed over her like waves, each one bearing some new thought or product or emotion, until she was waterlogged.

She soon understood that in order to function as a human in this new world she would need a number of *devices*. A tablet, or two, or three. A messenger. A card that held credits upon it. Another that identified her.

The last two could be replaced by something called a wrist chip, but that seemed an enchantment beyond her means. It would be simpler to conjure up cards than to try to work out the intricacies of imbedding the information into her skin.

She was about to turn away when a feature flashed upon the nearest screen. It showed a large collection of youths attending a sporting event. Attention sharpening, she concentrated on the image, ignoring the uniformed players running about the green field in favor of observing the crowd.

*This!* This was what she sought. A concentration of people young enough to be susceptible to the mark of magic, yet old enough to be able to move about the world without a chaperone.

Using her magic, she nudged that screen's volume up until she could hear.

"...and once again a disappointing night for Crestview High, as the Cougars lose their third straight game of the season."

Now she noticed the large letters inscribed at the edge of the field, spelling out *Crestview High School*.

Once she obtained the items she needed for her existence in the human world, she had a new goal. Whatever a high school might be, she would discover how to enter it and become a student there. It was the perfect place to carry out the Dark Queen's mission.

HOURS LATER, bewildered and bedazzled from spending so much time in front of the screens, Brea floated beneath the orange-washed clouds obscuring the night sky and let the breeze bear her back to her shelter.

The stained floor and broken windows made it seem a hovel compared to the riches she had just seen. Yet it was *her* hovel. And unlike the glass palaces of the shops, here she could feel the wind as it blew in through the half-collapsed roof. The stars, when they shone, were visible overhead, and the rain and dew could enter as they willed.

Wearily, she let herself become solid flesh. She had over-taxed herself. After staggering to fetch a cup of water, she curled up in the middle of the floor, but sleep eluded her. Instead, hyper-colored visions flashed through her mind, a montage of everything she had seen upon the screens.

Tomorrow, she must set about establishing herself in the mortal world. At least she knew where to begin—with gear and clothing and a reconnaissance of the place called Crestview High…

Sleep overtook her like a fast-moving hawk, catching her up in its claws all unawares. When Brea next blinked, morning light lay sluggish across the floor, mirroring her own state.

Sighing, she fetched water, then stepped outside. The dead tree beside her sagging doorway rustled, as if in sympathy. She was tempted to nurture it, to pour her magical energy into its restoration—and in another time and place, she would have.

But the queen's geas lay heavy upon her. There would be no squandering her small store of magic simply to rescue one tree.

Sipping from her broken cup, she let the pale sunshine warm her cheeks. Today, she would be herself. Not quite fey. Not quite mortal—but close enough to pass for one.

A temporary glamour would give her suitable clothing while she visited the palatial stores. As for the card full of credits, a quick act of duplicate conjury should do. Finesse the details with a nudge of magic, and she would be able to purchase whatever she needed.

Transporting everything might prove more difficult, but sometimes plain effort was the better choice. She could conserve her energy if she hand-carried her purchases back into the Exe. Of course a touch of concealment would be in order, but that was far easier than trying to magically transport items from one place to another.

A breath of wind, a shimmer of light, and a hidden alleyway later, she emerged on the street full of shops. Cautiously, she shot glances at her reflection in the windows as she passed.

Her dark hair held a sheen of silver, which she quickly muted. For her illusion, she wore the type of trousers called *jeans*, and a gray sweater that matched the color of her eyes. Her skin was pale, but not remarkably so. She appeared to be a normal girl, of an age termed a *teenager* in the modern world.

Holding her head high in an attempt to look as though she belonged, Brea entered the enormous shop she had explored the day before. Her first task was to mirror-magic one of the cards so that she could procure the items she desired.

Under the guise of perusing a display of handbags, she sidled close to the purchasing area. When the next customer handed her card to the shop girl, Brea closed her eyes in concentration and hummed beneath her breath. A moment later, a silvery card appeared in her hand. Fortunately, it was not made of metal but of the material the mortals called plastic, which seemed to be everywhere.

Brea tapped her index finger three times upon the card, imbuing it with endless credits, the name *Brea Cairgead*, and the attribute of unquestioning acceptance. The effort left her a tiny bit dizzy. She would need to stock up on bottles of water to carry with her for replenishment.

"Are you all right, miss?" A man wearing the uniform of

store security paused beside her. Concern and suspicion mixed in equal parts in his expression.

"I am well." She made sure to flash the card at him. "Just a trifle hungry."

"Gotta watch that low blood sugar." He nodded knowingly. "Restaurant three doors down."

"My thanks." The word tripped on her tongue, but he didn't seem to notice. In the Realm of Faerie, one did not bestow thanks, for it was an obligation and an unwelcome debt laid upon the recipient.

Yet it was customary in the human world, and her mission was to become as human-seeming as possible. Affixing a smile to her face, Brea went outside, aware that the guard watched her depart. It was for the best to test the card away from his suspicious gaze, in case her magics had gone awry.

The small café down the block was a tranquil haven, paneled in dark wood with actual, living plants decorating the wide windowsills and a tiny fountain playing near the door. She let out a sigh, then hovered awkwardly, unsure of the protocol.

"Go ahead and take a seat anywhere," the serving girl said, waving one hand.

Brea chose a table beside the window, where the airy brush of ferns against her arm steadied her even further. It was frightening, being out in the world and interacting with mortals. She half-expected them to point and scream, decrying her as inhuman and then doing something barbaric, like tying her to a stake to be burned alive.

She shuddered at the thought of such a hideous fate and attempted to distract herself by reading one of the colorful menus stacked upon the table.

"Herbal tea and a bowl of soup, please," she said when the bespectacled serving girl came to inquire.

The tea would be lovely, and she would pretend to eat the soup. She would take no mortal food, only pure liquids infused with flowers and leaves. Indeed, when the soup arrived, the scent of it made her feel ill. It would provide excuse enough for her to linger, however, so she pushed the bowl to the side and concentrated on the steam wafting up from her tea.

Spearmint and chamomile, which grew in the meadows on the brighter edges of the Dusk Vale. The scent made a wave of longing rush through her. Would she ever return again to the stream she called home, or leap and splash in the silvery waters of the nearby lake?

Such thoughts had no profit to them, and she resolutely turned her mind away.

And if there was an echo of loneliness to the idea of returning to her existence in the vale, what of it? She was a solitary fey, needing no companionship except the dragonflies to dance with and the ripples of wind on the water to sing her to sleep.

"Anything else?" the serving girl asked as she passed Brea's table.

Brea shook her head and handed the girl the silver card, willing her fingers not to tremble. If the worst happened, klaxons sounded and guards appeared, she could always disappear into a mist and float away.

Trying not to appear obvious, she watched the serving girl swipe the card. Nothing dire occurred, and Brea let out a tiny, relieved sigh.

"Thanks for coming in!" the girl said, returning her card and a printout.

"My pleasure." Brea rose, then hesitated.

From the dozens of vids she had absorbed the night before, she understood it was customary to leave a token of thanks at the table.

With a thought, she conjured up a few coins and nudged them next to the plate. She hoped they would not turn to leaves the next morning, in the way of faerie gold. But since she had no actual money, the deception couldn't be helped.

Confidence quickening her stride, Brea went back into the glass palace of wonders and proceeded to purchase everything she found both beautiful and useful. A velvet coverlet the color of sapphire-blue water, a set of pure crystal drinking goblets, a small chest with bronze fittings, two pillows filled with goose-down, and, more for fancy than practicality, a string of colorful glass baubles to hang from one of the broken-out windows.

Her cart was full—overfull—and she had not begun to select her wardrobe. It would be difficult enough to carry this much back to her hideout in the Exe, so she made herself stop. Only then was she aware of the weariness pulsing through her. The lights overhead seemed suddenly far too bright, searing her eyes, and she wanted to curl up on one of the display beds and sleep.

Instead, she scraped up the strength to finish making her purchases, then lugged the bulky bags out of the shop.

Back on the sidewalk, the hum of metal assailed her. More vehicles traveled the street now, and her reserves had fallen too low. Oh, curses upon her small store of strength, so quickly depleted! She staggered to the end of the block and halted, her chest rising and falling with the beginnings of panic.

No, she would not crumble and weep. Had she not already proved she was strong enough to face the human world? She must simply be more clever.

Tipping her face to the sky, she hummed a rhyme of lightness, of ease, and the bags she carried lifted, each one weighing no more than a vial of moon dust, a spiral of silk.

Exhaustion pulled at her, but she made herself walk sure and straight down the streets until she reached the squalid alleyways bordering the Exe.

Then, with the last droplets of her strength, she tugged a concealing enchantment over herself. By the time she gained the safety of her shelter, she was weaving and stumbling like the town drunk.

Nearly weeping with relief, Brea dragged herself over the threshold and set her bags on the floor. Her wards of protection emitted a serene silver glow, showing that no one had breached the boundary while she was away. It was all she could do to pull the coverlet out of its bag and wrap herself in it before she plummeted into exhausted sleep.

THE SUN CHASED the moon across the sky four times before Brea awoke fully. She lay upon the floor, reveling in the softness of azure velvet pulled up around her chin, and stared at the evening-shrouded sky visible through her half-broken roof. A strange feeling washed through her, different from the simple acceptance of things she felt when in her waterbound form. If she had to name it, she might call it *contentment*.

Ah, it was dangerous, to feel such things as a mortal again. She must harden herself, for she could not afford any more weaknesses.

As shadows stole into the room, she fetched her customary cup of water, drinking from the delicate edge of one of her new goblets. She cast a small golden ball of light for illumination while she unpacked the bags, hung her sun catcher in the window, then pulled out the bronze-bound chest.

She let three drops of water run off her fingers, each one imbuing an enchantment into the wood: protection, concealment, safekeeping. Carefully, she placed the medallion into the chest, then closed it and murmured a word of binding. Blue lines flared, and the magic was set.

The chest went into the corner, her new bedding pulled beneath the intact portion of the roof, her set of goblets arrayed in the bathing room. It was a start, and a good one at that.

Now she must attire herself with human clothing and, even more essential, purchase at least one screen device, that center of the much-changed mortal world.

As she had done before, Brea floated to the area where the shops were, then transformed herself into human form. She entered a shop with garments on display, and soon discovered the immense frustration of having to find clothes of the proper size and shape.

Cloaking herself in starlight and mist was so much simpler! Illusions did not tug or squeeze or hang imperfectly upon her form the way physical clothing did. It took the better part of the day just to assemble a few outfits, when she had envisioned being able to complete her entire wardrobe in a few simple hours.

Unlike the first time she had attempted to shop, she monitored her energy levels. When tiredness began to tug upon her bones, Brea completed her purchases and took them back to her shelter.

She did the same the next day, and the next, and her possessions grew: clothing of all kinds, jewelry, a small store of cosmetics, scavenged boxes to keep her new belongings in, and an increasing collection of tablet devices.

She found herself fascinated by them—those small flat screens holding such power and magic. The Brea of her past would have thought such things darkest sorcery, and indeed both the mortal and fae parts of herself were dazzled and a little frightened by the technology. *Tech*, as the humans called it.

It was beginning to make sense, how the simulation game called Feyland had intersected with the Realm of Faerie. One type of magic meeting another, in a place that was neither real nor unreal, and anything was possible. No wonder the Dark Queen was determined to pull as many mortals as she could into her dying Realm. Their dreams, their sorrows, their blood would revitalize the land.

Brea shivered at what that ultimately meant to the humans and their world. But despite her qualms, she was bound to do the queen's bidding.

Still, she delayed. Before she embarked upon her mission, she must find one more pair of soft leather boots, and an amulet made of amber to match the bracelet she had procured the other day. New tablets were announced, and surely she could not begin her work for the queen until she was outfitted with the newest devices.

She had been in the mortal world a fortnight, and that

first, warm kernel of contentment was beginning to grow into something more. A sensation she had all but forgotten. Happiness.

*Perhaps you might simply stay here,* a small, treacherous part of herself whispered. *Do not return to the Realm, do not put your touch upon the humans. Just make this tiny, perfect life for yourself.*

It was tempting, and yet she knew it would never succeed. Beyond the fact that some nights loneliness still shrouded her in a cold fog, the Dark Queen would not turn a blind eye to Brea shirking her duties.

She had been sent to the human world to make youths susceptible to the magic of the Realm, so that when they played Feyland they would slip and tumble into the queen's clutches instead of staying safely within the confines of the game. Here, in the city of Crestview, mortals had already crossed that boundary more than once, making it more permeable and easier to bend to the Dark Queen's wishes.

Brea was but a tool in the queen's implacable hand.

The next morning she awoke with the aftermath of frightening dreams still shivering through her. Redcap goblins had chased her through the Exe, the queen had stared at her until she had felt a blackthorn dart through her heart. Clutching her chest, Brea had felt hot blood flow through her fingers.

The warnings were clear. She must not delay any further.

Brea flicked on her newest tablet and typed out the words of her next, inevitable step. *How to become a high school student.*

Twenty minutes later, with a touch of enchantment humming inside the system, she had an identity as an exchange student from Ireland staying with a fictitious host family. With a last tap upon the screen, the deed was done. She was now enrolled as a junior at Crestview High—and expected to begin classes the very next Monday. Fear shivered through her at the thought.

But had she not used her wits and small magic to succeed among the mortals? As daunting as this next part of her mission might be, she would face it and show the Dark Court that she was not a helpless creature to be gutted and tossed aside.

She was a faerie girl. Whether the human world knew it or not, she would put her mark upon it—silvery and magical, shining with the light of a hundred invisible stars.

*FIND out more about Brea's quest in ROYAL, Book 5 of the Feyland series...*

# OTHER WORKS

## THE FEYLAND SERIES

*What if a high-tech game was a gateway to the treacherous Realm of Faerie?*

THE FIRST ADVENTURE - Book 0 (prequel)

THE DARK REALM – Book 1

THE BRIGHT COURT – Book 2

THE TWILIGHT KINGDOM – Book 3

FAERIE SWAP - Book 3.5

TRINKET (short story)

SPARK - Book 4

BREAS'S TALE - Book 4.5

ROYAL - Book 5

MARNY - Book 6

CHRONICLE WORLDS: FEYLAND

FEYLAND TALES: Volume 1

## VICTORIA ETERNAL

*Steampunk meets Space Opera in a British Galactic Empire that never was...*

PASSAGE OUT

STAR COMPASS

STARS & STEAM

COMETS & CORSETS

**THE DARKWOOD CHRONICLES**

*Deep in the Darkwood, a magical doorway leads to the enchanted and dangerous land of the Dark Elves~*

ELFHAME

HAWTHORNE

RAINE

**SHORT STORY COLLECTIONS**

TALES OF FEYLAND & FAERIE

TALES OF MUSIC & MAGIC

THE FAERIE GIRL & OTHER TALES

THE PERFECT PERFUME & OTHER TALES

COFFEE & CHANGE

MERMAID SONG

# ABOUT THE AUTHOR

Growing up on fairy tales and computer games, *USA Today* bestselling author Anthea Sharp has melded the two in her award-winning, bestselling Feyland series. She loves to write immersive fantasy and fantastical worlds full of adventure and a touch of romance.

Anthea makes her home in sunny Southern California, where she eats fresh citrus, plays the fiddle, and writes up a storm. Contact her at antheasharp@hotmail.com or visit her website – www.antheasharp.com

Anthea also writes historical romance under the pen name Anthea Lawson. Find out about her acclaimed Victorian romantic adventure novels at anthealawson.com.